The DOCTOR, the CHEF or the FIREMAN

BY

DEBBIE K. LUM

Library of Congress Control Number: 2017902096

DKLit, LLC, Tampa, Florida

ISBN-13: 978-1-944463-09-0

Interior formatting by Tugboat Design

www.debbielum.com

Acknowledgments

When I travel on airplanes, story ideas pop into my head. And since I flew over thirty flights last year, I had plenty of time to think. While I do my story conceptualizing in the air, it is the help of my friends that keeps me grounded.

Pat Trecker, thank you for the early advice.

Kathryn Barry and Marta Vittini, welcome to my beta reader club.

Keri Riegler and Amber Marcellino, this journey would be no fun without you.

Sarah Wilson Thacker, for a super fresh book trailer.

Mandy Schoen, an amazing editor.

And Jill Reagan Healey, thank you for your steady hands as you continually pick me off of the floor.

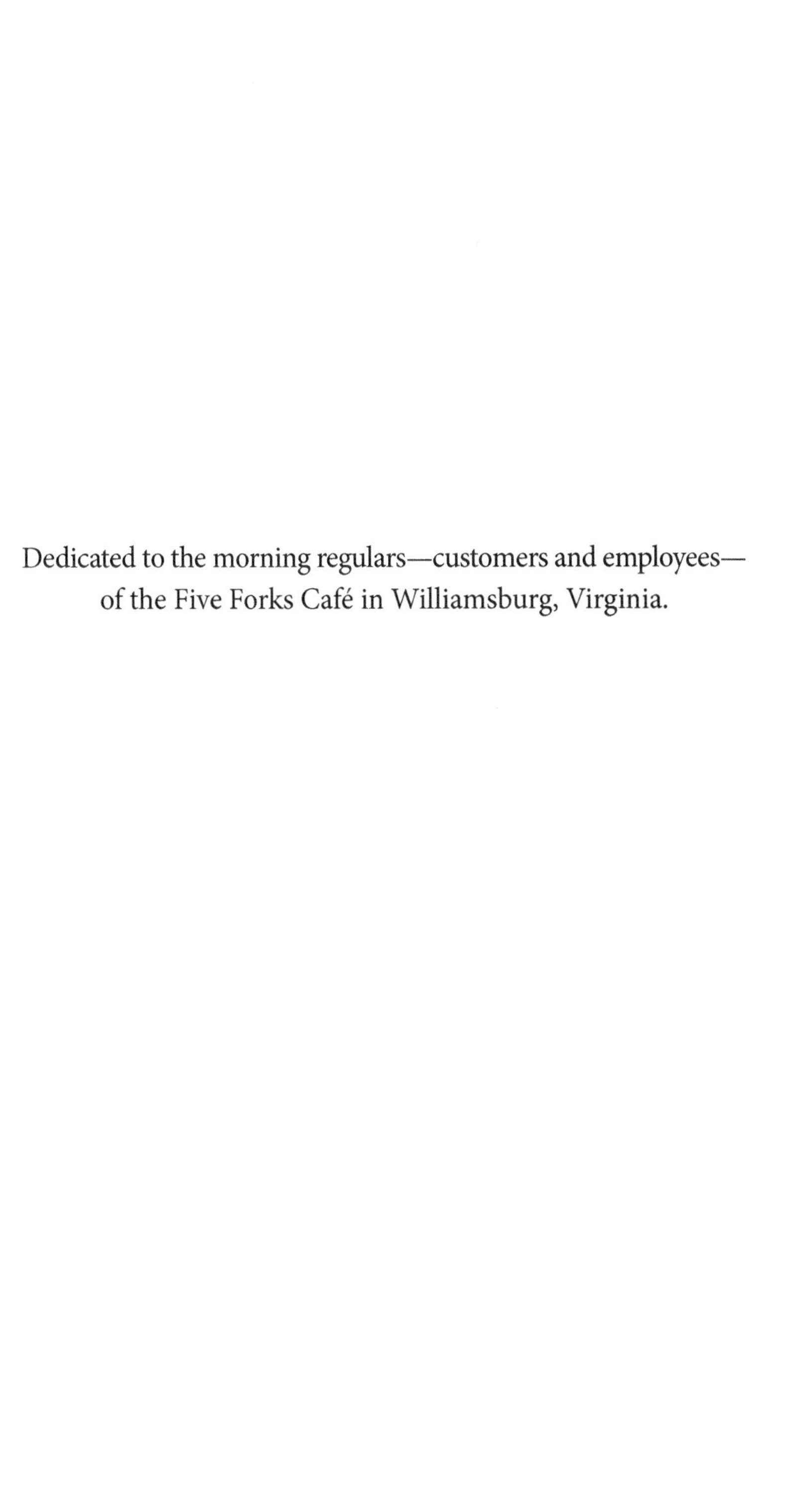

Dedicated to the morning regulars—customers and employees—
of the Five Forks Café in Williamsburg, Virginia.

[ONE]

Afternoon sunlight softly filters though the apartment blinds. Kendra King sets her hands on her hips and sweeps her eyes over her new kitchen. Cardboard boxes cover the small floor. Only a corner of the granite counter can be seen from under the wads of opened packing paper.

Which box to open next?

The thought, and the heavy cardboard smell, are enough to make her sick.

She closes her eyes. The soft sunlight warms her skin. The quiet steadies her. Finally she's standing upright in her upside-down world.

Her apartment door rattles and her eyes fly open. She fists her hands as the door swings open.

"Good news: they had the brisket!" says Davis Perkins. He steps inside and plops a paper to-go bag on the counter, his smile and eyes as wide as if he'd won the lottery. "This will pick you up! I've never known you to turn down barbecue."

She cracks a half smile. "Saved by the brisket. And by you. Thanks again for driving with me from Richmond today." She steps around him and locks the door.

"Anytime." He unpacks four disposable foam containers and looks up, his brown hair as tousled as usual and his pale blue, button-down shirt uncharacteristically untucked. "No, I didn't mean that. Not anytime. Only one time. One done-and-run rescue per life."

Kendra nods. She's only twenty-six years old. Who would have thought she'd need a done-and-run rescue this early in life? "So what's the big deal about the brisket anyway?" She leans over Davis's shoulder as he tears open a plastic sauce packet.

"Seven Spoons runs out early if you don't get there by like six p.m." Davis shoves a forkful of brisket into his mouth and his eyes slowly roll. "Heaven. Just…heaven."

She smiles. Right now food is the best kind of distraction. "So, this Seven Spoons place is one of your new favorites, huh?"

"Hell yeah. Cory City's finest dive! It was the first place Susan took me to…to you know…seal the deal and convince me to move here."

"Smart girl. Now when you get married, she'll have the five-minute commute and you'll be stuck with the hour drive to Richmond."

"Worth it," he says, smothering his next bite with sauce.

Her eyes lower to the floor. "Do you think…you know… what I did today was worth it?" She slowly looks up to him.

Davis's brisket-and-sauce covered fork freezes mid air. "Packing up and moving out while your boyfriend was still at work? I guess it depends on what really happened between you two. And since you haven't told me what really happened…"

"I know. I can't."

"It doesn't matter what I know, as long as you are righting

a wrong, or keeping yourself safe, or following your heart." He takes his bite of brisket.

She nods. *It's all three.* "Thanks for always having my back."

"Back at ya," he says, digging in for another bite.

Kendra's eyes tighten. "Hey, why are there four containers? I thought only Susan was coming after work."

Davis nods, his mouth full. "She's bringing a friend to help unpack," he mumbles, then swallows. "Only, we already got everything in so I don't think you need more help."

Kendra looks around her space. Help? The two folding chairs they picked up at a drug store on the way here to Cory City will be fine until she finds a couch. The bed she ordered over the phone will be delivered within the hour. Her tablet plugged in on the counter is serving quite well as a stereo at the moment. She'll unpack her three suitcases stuffed with clothes sometime later tonight. There isn't much here, but her mind is already racing with decorating ideas she saw in last month's *Elle Décor* magazine. And the big plus is she's the only one who can lock her door. Right now, she doesn't need unpacking help. The help she'd rather have is emotional.

Three soft knocks sound on the door. "Y'all in there?" a woman's voice with a slight southern accent asks.

Kendra unlocks the door and flings it open, smiling. "Finally!"

Susan Porter squeals and squeezes Kendra tight. "Oh God," Susan says. "I can't believe this has happened but I'm so glad you're here…and living in the same building as us!" She pulls back, repositioning her hands on Kendra's shoulders. "Are you okay? Have you talked with him? What's going on?"

Kendra swallows hard. *Careful what you say.* "I'm hungry.

That's all I really want to say." She adds a fake smile to convince Susan to switch topics.

Susan swings her straight, long blonde hair from her face. "Sorry, but you know I have to know more. I've already gotten three calls."

"What? Christopher? He already called you? Are you kidding me?"

"Hey, hey," Davis says, stepping away from his meal. He plants a kiss on Susan's lips. "Baby, let's eat first and then talk about the doctor from hell. Hey, look," Davis says, smiling and pointing toward the kitchen counter. "Seven Spoons brisket!"

Her shoulders drop as she exhales. "I just want to help."

Davis pulls her closer, wrapping his arms around her petite body. "You're here," he whispers, rubbing her back. "We are helping."

Kendra watches their embrace, feeling awkward and empty. She sighs and collapses into one of the folding chairs. *This will never work.* Christopher Randall will come after her. Cory City isn't far enough away. Susan is like a human breadcrumb leading him right to her. And the deal she made with him? It'll never last. *Oh God, why did she ever fall for him?* How did she get sucked into his well-to-do world? Into his dreamy promises of forever? Was it his potential, since his career was locked-in as a doctor? Or his tight, fit body that gave her those long nights of mind-blowing love? *Oh shit; that's why.*

Davis strokes his hand slowly down Susan's back and Kendra decides it's time to remind them she's still in the room.

"What did you tell Christopher when he called?" she asks.

Susan pulls away from her fiancé. "He didn't call. Big sis did. Three times."

Crap, not Portia Randall. Three years older than Christopher, Portia has enough bitch power to fuel evil in an entire college sorority. Watching anyone try to stand up to her is like watching someone run into a table saw. And there's nothing she protects more fiercely than her little brother.

"I still don't understand why you two are friends," Kendra says.

"It's hard for me not to like everybody," Susan says, smiling. "Even Portia. She's okay, really, once you get to know her. It's easier for me, I guess, since she and I go way back."

"So what did you tell her?"

"I told her I'd see you tonight and if I knew more, I'd tell her," Susan says.

"No, don't. Tell her nothing, please," Kendra says, getting up.

"But I just…"

Davis touches Susan's arm. "Let's eat."

Kendra steps to the counter, tugging up her size four jeans that have become loose after she'd barely eaten this past week. Right now though, this incredible, smoky barbeque smell is totally calling her name. She opens her to-go container and picks up a mini loaf of cornbread, still warm. Her first bite makes her eyebrows rise. *Dang!* A buttery soft corn flavor rushes through her mouth and with one bite all of her problems seem to disappear. Screw the brisket, this cornbread is heaven! Maybe life in Cory City is worth a try. After all, she landed a promotion when she transferred positions at the bank. Tomorrow she begins her new job and her new life. It's time to stop running. It's time to move forward. What difference does it make anyway if Christopher finds her? She's not going back to him. He lied. She caught him. And she can't live a life of lies. As long as the police don't knock on her door, the secret she's keeping will stay just that: a secret. And as long as he keeps up his end of their deal, she'll keep up hers.

A strong knock sounds on the door, making Kendra gulp down her cornbread.

"That must be my friend," Susan says.

Kendra steps to the door. Cautiously she opens it and her eyes slowly widen with curious joy as if she were visually unwrapping the best gift ever.

Cowboy boots, jeans and a fitted white t-shirt struggling to cover a chest full of muscles. His chiseled smile is the sexy centerpiece of his smoothly shaven face and his perfectly wavy brown hair is so perfectly styled she can't think of any word other than perfect.

Forget the brisket and cornbread.

Kendra is face-to-face with heaven.

[TWO]

"Kendra?" the man asks, smiling and standing outside her door.

Heaven speaks. "Um, yeah…" she says, her face feeling frozen but her body suddenly hot from the neck down.

"Matt!" Susan says, rushing up behind Kendra. He steps inside to give Susan a quick hug. "Thanks for coming!" she says. "Kendra, Matt! Matt, Kendra."

"Matt Livingston," he says to Kendra, hand extended. "Nice to meet you."

Kendra grips his hand, his touch so strong and reassuring, and gives him a friendly shake. "Nice of you to help me move in."

Matt looks around. "Your apartment layout is different than mine. This is one bedroom, right?"

"Only one. You live here too?" Kendra asks.

"First floor. Because of Gracie," he says, smiling warmly.

"Your…girlfriend?"

"Ha—yeah—the love of my life right now. She's my yellow lab."

A daydream flashes before Kendra's eyes: she and Matt,

hand-in-hand, Gracie playfully romping between them, a fall chill in the air as they walk down a leaf-strewn path—no—a leaf-strewn sidewalk leading to Seven Spoons, where the cornbread stays warm and the brisket never runs out…

"Kendra?" Matt asks.

She shakes her head, abandoning her dream. "I'm afraid I don't have much here for you to help with."

"Come eat!" Davis says, opening Matt's to-go container. The two share a bro-shake and Matt rips open a sauce packet and pours sauce over his meal.

"Never had time for lunch today, so this is a real treat," Matt says. "Had another busted hydrant down on Travis Street. Second one this week."

"What the heck?" Davis says.

Kendra cocks her head. "Where do you work?"

"At the fire station off of Route 5. I'm a firefighter," he says, wiping some stray sauce from the corner of his still-smiling lips. Her stomach flutters watching him. "Sorry about eating so fast. I don't mean to be rude," he says.

Kendra pats his shoulder. "Not at all—eat!" *Eat. Stay. Move in with me.* She squeezes her eyes closed and walks to the refrigerator. Gee, she's been without a boyfriend for eight hours and is already acting like a horny teenager. *You don't need a new relationship. Stop it.*

"What's up with the hydrants around here?" Davis asks. "I couldn't drive down Travis the other day because of the gushing water."

Matt nods. "Years of neglect, thanks to my boss."

"Who's that?" Kendra asks.

"Rip Edwards, the fire chief," he says sarcastically.

"Been here forever," Susan says, "like my boss, Tony Fletcher, the mayor."

"It won't take you long to see," Matt says, "this is their town and we just live in it. And pay them taxes to fund their pet projects."

"Sounds like a classic, old, small town," Kendra says.

"Classic, old, small, corrupt town," Matt adds, taking another bite of brisket.

"Hold on. I'm not sure being stupid means they're corrupt," Davis says.

"You're new here too," Matt says, eyes darkening. "Just wait. Something will happen to you or you'll see something and you'll know what we mean."

Kendra gazes at Matt. His expression is alert, his posture strong. His clenched jaw says determined but his smile says loving…and caring. "Well, who knows," she says. "Maybe the old guy will retire and you'll be fire chief one day."

He holds up his arms in victory. "There it is! My life's goal perfectly read by someone I just met a minute ago!" He pulls her into a hug. "The woman of my dreams. Marry me already."

Her knees buckle and she squeezes him back. Tightly.

"Well, that escalated quickly," Davis moans.

Kendra pulls away, staring into Matt's deep-brown eyes. "We should date first, before we marry," she teases, poking him in the chest.

"You should unpack first, before we marry," he says, looking around.

Ugh. One glance around the room and that helpless feeling returns. *Christopher. Her run. The risk…* She reaches for a box but Matt reaches it first. "Let me get that," he says, picking it up and placing it on the counter. Kendra pops the box open and Davis peeks inside.

"I knew it. I told you to pitch these," Davis says.

"What?" Kendra reaches inside the box and pulls out a handful of magazines. *Elle, Glamour, Vogue, Harper's Bazaar.* "Fashion is my hobby. These subscriptions aren't cheap so I'm not throwing them away."

"You've got, like, the last six months of every magazine here!" he says, looking through the stack. "Lighten the load."

"Duh…the spring clothes are in these fall editions. You have to keep old editions to keep up, my fashion-needy friend."

He leafs through an issue of *Vogue* and stops on a page with a clothing ad. "Wow, those are nice," he mumbles, his full attention on the magazine.

Kendra leans in. The full-page photograph has a man and a woman, embracing, standing on the edge of a rock-strewn cliff, a beautiful ocean view behind them. The woman's acid-washed denim jacket is on point, as is the man's fitted blue, rolled sleeve, button-down shirt. "What's nice? What the guy's wearing or the girl?"

"Those." He points to the man's shoes.

She shakes her head. "No, never, no."

"I've always wanted a pair of blue boat shoes."

"No. Can't let you, like ever," Kendra says. "Unless you live in New England and you are tending to your yacht. In the summer."

Matt grins and picks up an issue of *Elle.* "Do you want to be in these magazines or just have what's in them?"

Be in these magazines? *Right.* At five feet, five inches tall she'd be a pretty short model. At least she's brunette, like most models she sees in her magazines today. But while those models seem statuesque and perfect, she feels more down-to-earth and imperfect.

"I don't think I could ever—ever—be in these. But I like style. And stylish things." Kendra glances toward Susan and what Susan is sitting next to: Kendra's Louis Vuitton handbag.

Susan follows Kendra's eyes and then she rolls hers.

"Her ex bought her this," Susan blurts. "Costs as much as your next month's rent."

Kendra shrugs. Her Louis is her prized possession; a gift Christopher gave her on their one-week anniversary. She's wanted one since she was nine, when she and her mother first walked into a Neiman Marcus store. They had no business being there, but Neiman Marcus was a shortcut to the parking lot. Even though her father, the operations manager at the Richmond Motor Speedway, and her mother, who managed the ticket office, made a decent living, money became tight when her older brother decided to go to law school. There was no extra money for Kendra to splurge on Jack Rogers sandals in the summer or UGG boots in the winter. But looking is free and every change of season, Kendra wandered into Neiman Marcus to see the latest fashions. She'd fling two-thousand-dollar purses over her shoulder and squeeze her feet into the newest Christian Louboutin pumps. One day, she'll earn enough to buy her own. But is it bad to have a rich boyfriend give you good things now?

Matt clears his throat. "Your…ex?"

Kendra looks to the floor. "Long story."

"Well…now the wedding is off," he says, still wearing a smile. "I don't think I can keep you in the manner to which you are accustomed."

"Dang it," Kendra says, slapping her hands to her sides. "I just lost the man of my dreams, three minutes after meeting him and two minutes after he asked me to marry him." Her lips are clamped together but her grin is impossible to contain. A grin so contagious, Matt has it too.

Davis winces and puts down the magazine. "Well…now you are losing the friend of your dreams because it's time for me to go home." He nods to Susan. "Come on, baby. I think Kendra can take it from here."

Kendra breaks Matt's stare and turns to Davis, hugging him. His friendly hold wraps her with warm, reassuring memories. Davis has always been a brother-figure in her life, a family friend seven years older than her. He was her ride home every Friday when she was in fourth and fifth grade. He'd pick her up after he finished high school, the windows on his used Honda Civic rolled down and Elvis music blaring. She'll always remember the hug he gave her, like this, on the day she found out the guy she had a crush on chose someone else to take to the end-of-year dance. She was crying so hard in the after school pick up line she didn't even notice Davis's car pulling up to get her. He stopped traffic, got out and wrapped her in a hug that made all of the safety patrols, and even the mean Assistant Principal, smile. Who else but Davis could have guided her through this day? "What an incredible, messed-up day. Thank you for sharing it with me."

Davis gives her a squeeze. "All these years I've known you. It feels like your problems just keep getting better in a worse kind of way."

She pulls back and wrinkles her eyebrows. *Better? Worse? What?* She gives him a gentle slap on the shoulder and turns to

Susan. "Get your messed up fiancé out of here. You've got one week until the wedding to straighten him out."

Susan shakes her head, smiling, and pulls Kendra into her arms. "Hang in there. Every minute will get better."

Kendra opens the door and Davis and Susan step out. "And now for the ninety-second commute up to the fourth floor to get home," Davis says.

"I hope you make it safely," Kendra says as they walk away. "Watch out for busted hydrants!"

Matt has made his way to the door, his grin shy, his white t-shirt amazingly not covered in barbecue sauce despite how fast he ate his dinner. "I don't think I was much help here, but I sure enjoyed meeting you."

Her breath leaves her, which is probably good. If she had air in her lungs she might ask him to stay until her bed arrives and that request might not come out the right way.

"Listen." He steps closer, lowers his eyes and then looks back up to her. "Can I take you to dinner sometime this week? You know, to celebrate your move?"

Her weakened legs threaten to drop her to the floor. *Not a good idea. You always move too fast. You don't need a new love.* "I would absolutely love that."

He steps past her and now she's inches from his shoulders, his wavy hair, his gloriously perfect body. Surely he can feel her heartbeat racing.

"Welcome to Cory City," he whispers. "My life has just gotten incredibly better."

Time stops with his words. She inhales the deep scent of citrus and pepper from his cologne and whispers, "Mine too."

[THREE]

Lukewarm coffee sits on Kendra's desk and the snack-sized granola bar she ate for breakfast has her stomach doing the ready-for-lunch-now grumble. She feverishly types another email reply. The internal message announcing her promotion to Assistant Branch Manager for Oak Bank has filled her inbox with well wishes from colleagues. And since her morning was spent signing paperwork and meeting her new co workers, she's had little time to sit at her desk to work on replies.

Her phone lights up with a text. *Ah, Mom!*

Good luck on your first day of work today. Dad and I are proud of you.

Kendra quickly texts back:

Thanks! Love you both. Will talk to you soon.

"Excuse me, Kendra?"

Kendra turns in her chair to find Cindy, the proper and polite head teller, holding a vase bursting with orange and red roses.

"Whaaaat…is…that?" Kendra asks, putting her phone down and getting up. Must be from her former co workers at the West Richmond branch! She felt terrible leaving them so quickly, but her situation—and this great opportunity to get away—gave her little time for goodbyes.

Cindy places the flowers on Kendra's desk and Kendra reaches for the card and opens it.

I hope you are having a good first day at work.
But I hope our dinner tomorrow is better.
Matt

"Whoa," Kendra whispers.

"From…your boyfriend?" Cindy asks.

"From a guy, yes, but not my boyfriend," she says, tucking the card inside her purse.

"Well, whoever this guy is, he's got great taste. Beautiful fall colors too!"

"Kendra! Cindy!" a woman's voice barks. Branch manager Louise Danner stomps out of her office and stands tall with her hands on her hips. Her heavy, navy jacquard suit looks like it was fashionable, thirty years ago. "Someone needs to give Marley a break for lunch."

"But I'm heading out to my doctor's appointment now," Cindy says. "Remember? You gave me two hours off?"

Mrs. Danner grumbles. Nothing seems to please her; not even something she approved.

"I'll cover for Marley, no problem," Kendra says, stepping closer to Mrs. Danner. Kendra has yet to get the old lady to smile, even after giving her amazing, but fake, compliments all morning. Maybe Mrs. Danner can smell a lie. After all, surely Mrs. Danner knows her branch hasn't met their sales goals in over a year. She doesn't seem motivated to sell new loans, but sure seems interested in refinancing the same loans over and over again. And this branch's turnover rate is the highest in the region.

"I have a luncheon now," Mrs. Danner says curtly. "I will be back within two hours. Please keep everything running smoothly, as you are supposed to do." She swings her oversized purse over her shoulder and walks out a back door.

Okay, then. Kendra always treats her new employees to lunch on their first day. Evidently Mrs. Danner doesn't do the same. And actually, that might not be a bad thing. She's not sure what she would talk to her about while trying to eat a meal.

Cindy straightens. "I'll be back as soon as I can." Kendra nods and Cindy disappears out the back door.

Kendra steps behind the teller counter. Teller Marley smiles, her bright, floral peasant dress catching Kendra's eye. Kendra had noticed that dress from the Forever 21 fall dress collection too, but was worried it might be a bit too young for her. It's an adorable match for Marley though.

"I'm glad you're with us now," Marley says. "We needed a fresh face around here!" She locks her cash drawer and steps into the break room for her lunch just as an older woman walks into the branch.

"Well where the heck is everyone?" the woman asks from under a pair of oversized sunglasses, her sixties-inspired, teased gray hair piled high on her head. She, and the strong smell of her perfume, head Kendra's way.

"Hello," Kendra says. "May I help you?"

"You're new! What's your name, darling?" she asks, taking off her sunglasses with her slender, wrinkled hands.

"Kendra. I'm the new Assistant Manager."

"You're kidding me. Another one? What is Louise doing around here?" She leans forward on the teller counter, as if she's telling Kendra a secret, even though anyone in the lobby—if there was anyone else in the lobby—could have overheard her.

Kendra smiles, eager to complete this woman's transaction and move her along so she can breathe fresh air again. "How can I help you today?"

"Just depositing this." She slides a check and her driver's license forward and the motion pushes more of her perfume toward Kendra.

"Beautiful day outside, isn't it?" Kendra asks, stamping the back of the check.

"It is gorgeous. Fall is my favorite time of the year. You know, my husband and I got married in fall, right here in Cory City!"

"Really?" Kendra says, printing a receipt. "My good friend is getting married here next weekend. I guess they're following in your seasonal footsteps."

"You must mean Susan! Susan and her fiancé, Davis?"

"You know them?"

"Of course! My husband and I will be there at the winery this weekend. We wouldn't miss it for the world. You know, Susan works for my husband."

Kendra pauses. Susan works for the mayor, Tony Fletcher. She looks up at her computer screen and the account file that is still open. *Betty Fletcher.*

"Well then, Mrs. Fletcher, I will see you at the wedding this weekend," Kendra says.

Betty Fletcher smiles, slips her glasses back on her face and turns to walk away. "Please tell Louise I stopped by. She always loves to see me when I do."

"Of course. Have a wonderful day."

Betty and her perfume head out the door, leaving Kendra alone behind the teller counter. She opens her bank drawer again to straighten a messy stack of bills and pulls out the check she just deposited.

Interesting. It was a personal check, signed by Daisy Edwards, from the account of Rip and Daisy Edwards. *Rip Edwards?* He's the fire chief. Matt mentioned the mayor and his boss were close. But…

She looks again at the amount of the check.

Five thousand dollars.

* * *

Kendra snips another eight-inch strip of orange ribbon. "Almost out of orange," she says to Susan, letting the cut ribbon fall to the table.

Susan leans toward her to see. "I think one more spool of yellow and we'll have enough."

Kendra and Susan sit together at the table in Susan and Davis's apartment. Cut ribbons are piled in the middle of the table while boxes of sparklers are stacked on the table's edge.

"I don't know how I would have done this without you," Susan says.

"I'm so happy I can help, especially now that I'm here to help!" Kendra says. It's been awhile since she's had a friend like Susan. Her closest girlfriend was her college roommate at Richmond University and since they graduated she's barely had time to give her a call. Kendra had been lucky to land a management job at Oak Bank right after graduation and she had poured every waking second into her career. A few months later, Kendra met Christopher and was swept off of her feet and even further away from her girlfriends and her family. All of her emotional energy went to Christopher. She missed a girls' weekend planned by some of her college friends. There were dozens of declined dinner and coffee invitations. But when Davis introduced her to his new fiancée, she and Susan clicked. Maybe it's because everyone clicks with Susan. Or maybe it's because it finally clicked with Kendra that growing friendships is what had been missing in her life.

"This really is the least I can do, especially since I missed your bachelorette party last weekend," Kendra says.

Susan lowers her scissors. "You were fighting with Christopher that night, weren't you?"

Kendra stares down at her hands. "I'd really rather not talk about it." She opens the first box of sparklers, pulls one out and ties one orange and one yellow ribbon on the stick. She holds it up to distract Susan. "You want it like this, right?"

Susan's face lights up. "Perfect. Yes!"

"These will be so beautiful for all of us to hold when you guys leave the reception," Kendra says, picking up another sparkler. "Where did you get this idea?"

"Online and magazines and wedding expos…I've seen it all! I love all of these wedding event ideas. I've wanted to do this since the first time I saw it!" Susan points to two large stainless steel bowls on the floor. "Just put them in these bowls, stick side up, so people can easily grab them."

"Perfect." Kendra places the first one into a bowl. "How many more to go?"

"Two hundred and ninety-nine!"

"Wow, this is going to be a huge wedding. You really do know a lot of people, don't you?"

"Everyone is going to be there!"

Kendra looks down again, focusing on tying a ribbon. "I was wondering, you know, as a heads-up, if…"

"Portia hasn't told me yet if she's coming," Susan blurts. "I know things are stressful between you two."

Stressful? Try hateful. The last thing Kendra needs is the bitchy big sister of her ex to be at this wedding.

Susan continues, "Are you sure you won't even give me a hint why you suddenly moved out here?"

Kendra plops another finished sparkler into the bucket and gives a big exhale as she looks up. "Look, I found out something, okay? Something that Christopher is doing that is wrong. Really wrong. And I didn't want to be part of that, or him, or anything related to him or his family anymore. It's pretty simple but it's very complicated, if that makes any sense."

Susan fiddles with a bow. "And Portia has something to do with this?"

"She's the architect of mischief and that's all I want to say. I know someday she might pop up in my life again but right now, I don't want to see her. Or Christopher. I want to put as much time and distance between them and me as possible. I'd rather forget that I ever met the Randalls."

Susan shakes her head. "I don't get why people just can't get along."

"Not everyone can get along with everyone. At some point,

most people have disagreements. Except you and Davis, right?" Kendra smiles, trying to steer her off the subject.

"We had a big disagreement tonight, about this bachelor party he's having in Richmond. I know the guys will be drinking and I didn't think he should drive so far to get home but he didn't want to stay at the hotel. He said he wanted to be with me tonight and every night but I thought that was ridiculous."

"Well the hotel *is* his work, so he probably doesn't want to have the people who work for him check him in if he's drunk. And ridiculous? I think him wanting to be with you is more like romantic," Kendra says, plopping another finished sparkler in the bowl. "Speaking of romantic…"

Susan glances up. "Matt told me! He's taking you out tomorrow night!"

"That totally fell in my lap. So, you know him…what's he like?"

"Amazing! Handsome—well you can see that—but loyal, oh you two are going to hit it off."

"It seemed like we already did last night," Kendra says, smirking. "Is there any other scoop I need to know about him? You've known him awhile, right?"

"For years. He's dated a few people; girls I know. I've never really liked the girls he's gone out with, but you? I approve!"

Kendra's heart warms. The last thing she's looking for is love, but it never hurts to have the inside line on a guy. Especially before the topic of a second date even comes up.

"Hey," Kendra says, "I met the mayor's wife today at the bank."

"The Betty?"

"The Betty? Do you really call her that?"

"Yeah, everyone does. She's coming to the wedding."

"She mentioned that to me. She was telling me about her anniversary and then the wedding came up. You know, Matt doesn't think too highly of the mayor, or the fire chief. Do you?"

Susan lowers her eyes to her busy fingers. "I think it's time for some new ideas." Her face goes pale, eyes glued down. "I wouldn't be sad to see the mayor go."

The air feels thicker with her words. Kendra's gut tightens. Something is there. Something isn't right. She tilts her head to see Susan's face. Susan's eyes still look down, focusing as she ties a bow. "Hey," Kendra says. "You just made me spill the beans on Christopher. Why wouldn't you be sad to see Tony Fletcher go?"

Susan tosses a finished sparkler into the bucket and stands up. She makes her way to the kitchen and finds her empty wine glass from dinner, washed and beside the sink. She grabs the open bottle of wine and pours herself another glass. With her back to Kendra, she takes a long drink.

Kendra drops her ribbon, giving Susan her full attention. She and Susan may not have been friends for long, but Kendra can read girl code and this girl is sending an "SOS."

Susan pours more wine, her back still turned to Kendra.
Enough of this solo drinking.

Kendra crosses to the kitchen and slides her wine glass next to Susan's. Susan extends her pour into Kendra's glass, giving her the barest hint of a smile.

"Don't you ever tell Davis this," Susan whispers.

Kendra stiffens.

"Fletcher has been fresh with me." Susan takes another sip.

Kendra sips too.

"He grabbed me from behind once and I don't think it was

an accident. I go out of my way to avoid him now."

Kendra gently rubs Susan's back. "That's horrible. Did you report him?"

Susan shakes her head. "The head of HR is another good friend of The Betty's. Saying anything is hopeless. And I mean, I could have misread it. It may have been an accident. But still, it didn't feel right."

"Then why invite him and his wife to your wedding?"

"I have no choice, really. People would ask questions. Everyone who works for the city invites them to their graduations, weddings, holiday parties…it's just what everyone does."

Kendra takes another sip. "And Davis doesn't know?"

Susan shakes her head. "Please don't tell him. I don't want to risk anything happening before Saturday."

Kendra puts her glass on the counter. "Oh, Susan. Davis isn't going to not marry you because this happened! He'd support you. I know he would. He supported me when I was younger and guys were jerks to me!"

Susan shakes her head. "I don't want him to ask questions. I'll deal with it. I'll handle it. Like I said, I won't be sad the day Fletcher quits or retires, or…gets fired."

No. Not right. This jerk should be called out. But this didn't happen to her, it happened to Susan. And she has to respect her wishes. At least for now.

Susan's phone pings with an incoming text message. She reaches for her phone to read it.

"Davis is on his way back. He claims he's not drunk."

Kendra glances at her watch. It's ten p.m. "Early evening for a bachelor party, but I guess that's what you do when the party's on Monday night, huh?"

"Hey, thanks for listening," Susan says, one hand rubbing the back of her neck and her eyes drifting down to look at the floor.

Seems like they are both holding on to secrets. Maybe in time she'll tell Susan more about Christopher. And maybe in time, she'll learn if there's more that happened between Susan and the mayor. Because the way Susan just polished off her glass of wine and now broke eye contact, Kendra suspects there may have been more than a one-time "accidental" grab.

Kendra grips Susan's hand. "Anytime. But please, make sure you are safe, okay? Make sure this doesn't turn into something worse."

Susan looks up and nods, color rushing back into her cheeks. Her shoulders straighten and her smile brightens. "Trust me, it won't."

Kendra grins through closed lips. What a confident statement compared to such shyness a second ago.

With less than an hour until Davis gets home, they fly through their ribbon-tying project. Once three hundred are in the bucket, Kendra glances at her watch. "I'm out of here before he gets home and then you can say you did these all yourself!"

Susan and Kendra stand, and Susan gives her a hug. "Thank you again for helping. And for listening."

Kendra opens the door. "Saturday is going to be great. Relax and enjoy every moment."

"Oh I will. Don't worry! I've been imagining my wedding since I was a little girl. I'm going to enjoy every single minute!"

Kendra smiles and steps outside. "Goodnight," she says as Susan closes the door. She hears Susan flick the deadbolt lock. She slowly steps toward the staircase, wrapping her arms around her chest for warmth.

Breathing in the cold air sends a shiver down her spine. Yet, it feels good. Refreshing. This is the first time since arriving that she's been able to relax and take this all in.

Off in the distance, the moon's light reflects off of the river and into the sky like a glowing ball of light bouncing off of a mirror. Across the river, towering grain silos from a crop farm are the tallest buildings she's seen so far. From the aged red bricks of City Hall to the two-story, stained-glass windows on the Baptist church downtown, it seems that Cory City is a beautiful place. A small town isn't so bad. No one is rushed. People seem friendly, so far. The bigger accomplishment is she's actually here. She really did it. She stood up to Christopher and his family and said *enough*. The minute her promotion came through, she bolted. But she's not entirely free.

Kendra rests her hand on the cold, steel staircase handrail. She grips it for balance as she heads down the stairs.

She's got to get ready. She's got to stay ready. Christopher will find her. Portia too. And that's okay. As long as she's ready when they do.

But right now, she's not.

[FOUR]

Kendra leans against her open office door, a hand on her hip.

"Are you sure, Mrs. Dix?" she asks. "It only takes a minute to pre-qualify for a loan."

The tall, slender woman kindly smiles. "Well, not right now. It's only a dream of mine to have a condo on the Outer Banks. My husband would be very upset if he knew I was even telling you about this!"

"This is a good time of the year to apply," Kendra says. "You could close in time for the holiday and spend Christmas on the beach!"

"That would be lovely! All of my children and grandchildren will be here for the holiday and they would love the beach so much."

"Well, when you pick out your condo, please come back and see me."

"Yes, I definitely will."

Mrs. Dix turns for the exit and Kendra exhales. Another lost opportunity to sell a loan. At least chatting with Mrs. Dix gave her a reason to get up and out of her office. It's hard for her to see customers when they come in, which makes it harder to have a chance to talk with them. Her sales goals aside, she wants to meet people!

Marley giggles from behind the teller counter. "I'm going to ask for a long lunch one day so I can take you out for a good meal," she says to a man in front of her window.

Kendra steps around to see who she's talking to. He's an older gentleman, using a walker, wearing a World War II baseball cap. He's fiddling with his wallet, tucking a thick wad of bills inside.

"Oh, but then all the people in town will be talking about us," he says with a soft smile.

"Do you ever eat at home, Mr. Ellis?"

"Oh, sure, but I get better food when I eat at the nice restaurants."

"And you drink plenty of water, right?"

"About six glasses each and every day."

Watching their exchange warms Kendra's heart. That's what this place needs: more human-to-human interaction! There's something about this gentleman though. His quiet voice; his shaky hands stuffing his money into his wallet. He reminds her of her grandpa! And Marley is about as old as Kendra was when her grandpa died.

He's the only customer in the lobby and Marley locks her teller drawer and steps around the counter closer to him. She places her hand on his back as he steers his walker toward the door.

"Remember to eat more than only vegetables when you order your meal," she says, leaning closer to him. "Last night when I saw you at the restaurant, veggies were the only thing on your plate!"

"Oh, I get plenty of food. Don't you worry about me."

"Well, I think you need to eat more. You're looking a bit too tired for this early in the morning."

"Awww…I get plenty of rest. You have a nice day."

Marley pats his back and he slowly leaves, making his way into the parking lot.

"One of our regulars?" Kendra asks.

"Yes! Mr. Ellis has come here for years," Marley says, returning to her spot behind the teller counter. "He looked so tired when I saw him eating out last night. I couldn't help but mention it and make sure he's okay."

Kendra stands in front of the counter. "I love that we have such a good relationship with so many customers. We just need more of them here!"

"I agree," Marley says.

Mrs. Danner clears her throat. She's just opened the door of her office and is standing in the doorway with her arms crossed. "How can you be writing loans if you're not working in your office?" she grumbles.

"We have no loans in the pipeline right now," Kendra says. "But this morning I ran two demographic reports and have been looking to see where we could reach out to new customers."

Danner swirls her finger in the air, pointing around the lobby. "Well, wasting time gossiping with each other isn't going to get our work done."

Kendra straightens. This woman needs a serious boss boot camp retreat. The first session should be called "How To Be Nice To People".

"I'd like to see you at your desk, working on loans please," Danner says. She turns around, goes back into her office and closes the door.

Marley sighs. "She's always like this. Nothing makes her happy."

"That's okay." Kendra gets it, sort of. At least, she just read a great article in one of her magazines about how to deal with difficult bosses. The secret? Kill them with kindness and then over-perform. "You know, one good way to sell loans is to know your own customers. And if Mrs. Danner would prefer me sitting at my desk, well, that just gave me an idea on how I can do both."

Kendra glances into her office and then to an open space in the lobby. "Actually, a great idea."

* * *

The sun begins to dip below the horizon; today's cool, fall temperatures now even colder. Kendra sits alone inside a small cafe at an old, wooden table set for two. The end of a long, white linen tablecloth rests on her lap and her black knit dress. Every minute or so, her nervously shaking foot and her red Michael Kors pump peeks up from underneath the tablecloth. Two wine glasses are set on the table. One is half empty; the other waits to be filled.

Kendra sips her cabernet. What a lovely little Italian restaurant. But what a disappointing start to a first date.

A red-and-white checkered cafe curtain blocks some of her outside view, but a pair of headlights sweeping into the parking lot catches her eye. She peeks over the curtain to see a gray Chevy Silverado truck zip into the front space of the restaurant. Matt leaps out of the truck.

She folds her hands in her lap and watches him dash toward the restaurant door. His black oxford button down is tucked neatly into his dark-rinse jeans. He's wearing his cowboy boots again, and a belt with a large silver buckle completes his Virginia-cowboy look…a very attractive Virginia-cowboy look. He flings open the restaurant door, looking to the right and then quickly to the left when he sees her. Their eyes lock and smiles ignite. A few steps later, he's at her side and she stands to greet him.

"I can't believe that just happened," he says, his arms wrapping her in a warm, friendly hug.

She backs away, smiling. "Everything okay now?"

He pulls out her chair and she takes her seat again, then he sits across from her.

"Mr. Bakers is safe and back inside," he says, shaking his head. "Only the third kitten rescue of my entire career."

"Mr. Bakers? So adorable."

"He was, after I got him out of the tree. He wasn't so adorable when I was reaching between branches to grab him."

"How many children did you just save, by saving Mr. Bakers?"

"Four! It was a family over on River Street. Two boys and two girls all under the age of ten. Everyone was crying until I got him down."

"Well, if you are going to be late for a first date, rescuing a kitten is a damn good reason!" She lifts up her glass to toast him and he toasts her back with his empty glass.

"Looks like I need to catch up to you." The waitress arrives. "I'll have what she's having," Matt says to the waitress, who nods and leaves.

"Seriously," he says, looking back to Kendra and reaching over the table to hold her hand, his eyes softening. "Thank you for being patient. If the fire station wasn't so short staffed, I could've been on time."

"How many firefighters are here anyway?"

"Five!" He lets go of her hand and sits back. "When my grandfather was fire chief, there were ten full-time firefighters and that wasn't that long ago! Damn Rip and his cutbacks. Every year, he says there's no money for new hires. But every year, he seems to get something new."

"Like…"

"Like new office furniture last year. For *his* office! This year, he bought himself a new fire chief truck. Meanwhile, he's risking the safety of this city by giving us pennies."

"Too bad no one has called him out."

"Exactly. Sometimes I feel like I'm the only one who understands right and wrong. The mayor sure isn't going to do anything."

Kendra takes a sip of wine. *This guy wears his passion on his sleeve.*

He sits up straight. "Get this: the mayor and his wife, and Rip and his wife, took a fancy ski vacation together earlier this year. They were both off for three weeks!"

"And how much vacation do *you* get each year?"

"You catch on pretty quick," he says, smiling even though his eyes are clouded with disillusion. "I get two weeks, like all other city employees."

"Your grandfather used to be fire chief?"

His face brightens. "He's a legend at the firehouse. I've got my work cut out for me to get to his level but I'll do it. He challenged me, before he died, to follow in his footsteps. And I will. I'll get there."

Their conversation stops as the waitress delivers Matt's wine. "Are you ready to order?" she asks.

Matt looks to Kendra. "The lasagna tastes amazing. Want to try?"

Kendra looks to the waitress. "Two lasagnas, please."

The waitress leaves and Matt tilts his head. "I've been sitting here telling you about a kitten rescue and poor funding and bad boss stories and I haven't even asked you about your new job. How's it going?"

"Well," Kendra says, swirling her wine. "I sure haven't rescued anything as cute as a kitten but I did receive some beautiful flowers yesterday. Thank you."

"My pleasure," he says, smile wide.

"I also have two days' worth of bad boss stories. And I met the mayor's wife too."

"Ah, Betty! Around here, we call her 'The Betty.'"

"I heard that. You know her?"

"Everyone knows The Betty. Well, everyone knows her scent."

"No kidding. Once you get a whiff, she's hard to forget."

"What was she doing at the bank?" Matt asks, eyes alert.

"Routine business," Kendra says, and stops before saying anything else. It would be totally inappropriate for her to mention the check. Even though she's curious to get Matt's take on why his boss's wife just gave the mayor's wife five grand. "Anyway, enough about work. I think it's been exactly forty-eight hours ago that I met you."

"Best move-in experience of my life."

"Because you ate free food and didn't have to unpack anything?"

He laughs. "Because you were on the other side of that door." His smile is so wide his teeth seem to light up the table.

"And now, we're here."

"And now, I'm curious. Surely it wasn't just a new job that brought you to the great city of Cory City. What brings a woman like you to a small town like this?"

Kendra breathes deep and exhales. "A fresh start."

He raises his wine glass. "Okay then. To fresh starts."

She toasts his glass and they sip, eyes on each other.

"How long have you lived here?" she asks.

"Born and raised," he says. "I only moved away one time and that was to go to firefighting academy. I can't imagine myself anywhere else."

"Your dreams, your goals—they're all here?"

He smiles confidently. "I'll be fire chief, one day. Following my grandfather is what I've worked for my whole life. It's my destiny."

Love it. He has clear goals and knows right from wrong. He's not too manly to sip a cabernet even while wearing cowboy boots. And he's okay knowing his date will likely destroy the soon-to-be-served plate of lasagna. Heaven is perfect.

"What about you?" he asks. "What are your goals with this fresh start?"

She looks to her lap. *Her goals?* That's a deeper question than he might imagine. "When I graduated college, all I wanted to do was get away from Virginia. I grew up in Richmond, so, you know, anywhere near Richmond wasn't far enough. And look where I am now? An hour from Richmond." She musters a small laugh. "Seriously, though. I'm still figuring out my goals.

Really, I just want to have a good job, live in a beautiful space and surround myself with good friends and some fine and fancy things…"

The waitress arrives with two steaming plates of what looks like mounds of melted mozzarella cheese. Somewhere under there must be layers of pasta and ricotta. "Holy cow," Kendra says, watching the waitress place the meals in front of them.

"If you need anything else, let me know," the waitress says, then leaves.

"Like I said, this lasagna is amazing," Matt says. "But you didn't finish what you were saying…what you want after the fine and fancy things…"

Kendra stares at the steaming plate and then up to Matt's curious eyes. On the table may be the most delicious meal of her life. Across from her is a man who is confident, focused and super hot with his top three shirt buttons undone. Plus he looks strong enough to break down a door to save her if she were in trouble on the other side. And knowing one strong guy in town is not a bad thing, especially if Doctor Christopher Randall ever shows up. "What I want?" she whispers. "I just want to be happy."

If the cheese on her lasagna wasn't already melted, his smile right now would have melted it.

"Well, I'm not interested in fine and fancy things. But you being happy? I'd like to help you with that."

* * *

Two hours later, Matt and Kendra stand in the moonlit parking lot, leaning against his truck, laughing.

He points to the last car in the lot, a white Audi A3 convertible. "I take it that's your car."

"Good guess."

"Hmmm…looks like it needs to be washed, huh?" he says with a playful smile.

Thanks, Captain Obvious. The last thing on her mind as she ran away from Richmond was washing and waxing her ride.

"And this truck?" she says, peering into the dusty bed. "Whoa, what a mess!"

He leans over to see. "I'm a guy with a truck. It's supposed to be dirty." As he moves away from the truck, his face is suddenly a breath from hers. Their talking stops. The air thickens with anticipation and her heart rate quickens. A car drives by the restaurant and headlights sweep over Matt's face, illuminating the way his eyes are drinking her in. The car passes and silence covers the parking lot. He dips his head and his lips brush softly across hers in a kiss that is warm and sweet. Flutters unleash inside her body. He gently pulls back, but the sight of him, and the scent of his citrusy peppery cologne, keeps her flutters going.

"I'll wash my truck if you go out on a date with me again," he says, eyes twinkling.

She cracks a grin. "Deal. Although if you kiss me like that again, I won't care if your truck is dirty."

His eyes gloss over. "Deal." And his lips brush against hers again, softly, then he presses harder in a kiss that makes her head, her body, her entire world blur and spin.

Forget the doctor. She's falling head, feet, heart and soul—all-in for the fireman.

[FIVE]

Kendra flips down her car visor to block the rising sun, squinting just to be able to see the side of the road. Who knew that traveling east on Route 5 this early in the morning would feel like driving off of the earth and right into the sun? Also blocking her view is a blowing piece of paper under her windshield wiper, which she hadn't noticed until she started driving.

She finally approaches the turn she was looking for: the parking lot of the Seven Spoons Restaurant. Home of the famous brisket, Davis's favorite dive and "the" place in town for breakfast. A good, quick breakfast will help her get through her third day at work. Because chances are she won't have a lunch break again today.

Small potholes dot the parking lot and a white, wooden sign with large, red letters covers the front of the restaurant. She snags the last parking space up front and glances again at her watch. This place opened at 7 a.m. and it's already full by 7:10?

She turns off her car and steps out to remove the paper from her wiper, unfolding the handwritten note. A twang of fear stabs her gut. *Did Christopher find her already?* She holds her breath and reads.

I'll still wash my truck for our next date anyway.
No kittens will keep me from being late either. See
you tomorrow night.
Matt

Thank God. She relaxes, though reading Matt's note makes her feel those excited flutters again. She tucks the note in her purse and walks inside the restaurant. The soft jingle of bells tied to the door handle announces her arrival.

A scruffy old man sits near the door, alone at a round table for four, singing along to the Shangri-Las' *Leader of the Pack.* Wooden booths line the windows and the white, glazed-tile floor is so worn down, in some places you can see the orange porcelain underneath. No open tables or booths are available, unless she wants to sit at the table with the singing scruffy guy. A harried-looking waitress calls, "You wanna sit at the counter? We have a ten-minute wait otherwise."

"Counter is great, thanks!" Kendra says and takes a seat on a silver, round stool. This place looks like a worn-down version of the diner on the old television show *Happy Days.* Kendra holds on to her skirt hem to be sure it doesn't hike up as she takes a seat on the swivel stool and then she glances around. Two older men sit in a corner booth, waving their hands in the air, pointing at each other and laughing along with their stories. Another man sits alone in the booth next to them, quiet, pencil in hand, focused on the newspaper's crossword puzzle. For these guys, coming here every morning might be a regular part of their day.

And now that the song has changed to *Good Vibrations*, this may be the highlight of hers.

Three young men are busy working behind the counter: one as the master of the griddle, another handles the toast and muffins and the other plates up all the yummy food.

The waitress has both hands in the air, trying to quiet a large table of men, who look like golfers getting ready to head out for a round. "I can't get your orders if everyone is talking at once," she says. She turns her head toward the counter and hollers, "Nolan, baby, can you get her order?"

The master-of-the-griddle-guy glances over his shoulder. "You bet, my love," he hollers back.

He wipes his hands on a towel tied to his apron, still with his back turned to Kendra, and still focused on his griddle. His jeans look worn just right, a flawless fit to his perfectly rounded ass. Kendra tries not to stare. This guy might be dating that waitress, she guesses, from the friendliness of their exchange. And, well, it's kind of rude to stare at a stranger's ass. He's working quickly, moving cooked bacon from one side of the griddle to the other side. *Look at that.* He places the cooked bacon on a row of hamburger buns sitting on the clean side of the griddle. *Brilliant!* Bet that keeps the bacon hot without overcooking it, the bread absorbs the grease, plus he's probably using otherwise unusable stale hamburger buns.

Kendra blurts, "I like how you're using your buns!"

He spins around, eyes wide, his smile stretching across his face. His dimples crease into his cheeks as he puts one hand on his hip in a playful pose. "Why, thank you, stranger."

Kendra's face warms. "Oh, those…those buns…on your… hot cooking thing…" she stammers, pointing.

His dimples crease deeper with his smile. "Oh…right," he says, eyes lowered.

She buries her face in her hands. *Hilarious.*

"Would you like to order something, or just watch my buns?" he asks, pushing a menu toward her.

Is she a bad person if she wants to do both? "I better stick to breakfast, with no buns," she says, smiling. "What's good here?"

"Everything!" the scruffy man behind her hollers. She turns to see what he's eating: a pancake spread with butter and coated in syrup, with two slices of toast fully slathered in grape jelly lined up beside his plate. A few dollar bills are neatly stacked in front of his coffee. Bet he eats this, and does this, and spends the exact same amount of money, every single day. He waves his fork in the air. "But try the pancakes first. Any of them!" Then without missing a beat, he breaks out in a loud, off-key, falsetto voice to join the current song in progress.

Kendra turns to chef-awesome-jeans. "How about a pancake?"

His dimples are still on fire. "I'll make you blueberry." He turns back to his griddle, his jet-black hair and a hint of sideburn sticking out from under a navy blue baseball cap. He looks younger than her; maybe still in college? White order slips are clipped to a wire above his head. He reads each paper and then efficiently flies around the griddle, pouring pancake batter, turning eggs and flipping hash browns until they reach a golden brown. This must be the guy with the famous brisket recipe. And around here, he's probably a good guy to know, especially on days when you have a serious brisket craving and don't get here until after they've run out. Surely he keeps a little extra in the back, for special customers.

The waitress brushes Kendra's shoulder. "Did Nolan get your drink yet, honey?" she asks. She looks to be around Nolan's age too, with curly, blonde hair and a fresh, flawless complexion. They look like they'd be adorable together.

"Coffee, one cream and sugar would be amazing," Kendra says, noticing a man with a walker, wearing a veteran's World War II cap, slowly making his way to the door to leave. It's Mr. Ellis, one of the customers from the bank! Kendra slides off of her stool and steps to the door, just in time to open it.

"Why thank you, young lady," he says. He trembles as he walks, his face looking rather pale.

"Thank you for your service," Kendra says, watching him shuffle to his car, which is parked in a handicapped space, barely. At least he got most of his car within the blue painted lines of the space.

"Old man Ellis," the scruffy man says. "He doesn't look so good these days."

Kendra slides back on her stool, smoothing her skirt straight. Nolan stops his cooking and looks past her, out the windows to watch old man Ellis getting into his car. "I'm gonna go by his place and check on him later today," Nolan says, wiping his hands on his towel again.

"Does he live alone?" Kendra asks.

"Yeah," Nolan says, still looking past her, keeping an eye on Ellis. "No family. Except us."

"That's nice of you to care," she says.

He smiles at her. "I worry about him. There've been a couple of things going on around here. Something…something isn't right."

Her heart wants to help old man Ellis too. Maybe she can

make some soup and visit with him as well! Except, she doesn't know how to cook soup. Or where he lives. Plus, the man is a total stranger, other than he's an Oak Bank customer. But she can come back here tomorrow to see if he's okay.

Nolan places a plate in front of her. A steaming blueberry pancake covers the plate from end-to-end. On top he's laid out a few extra blueberries in the shape of a smiling face. She tilts her head and smiles at him. Nolan, with his dimples, smiles back.

One bite of the pancake makes her mouth dissolve with deliciousness. She's eaten nothing but good food since she arrived in town, but this? Hands down, blessed-blueberry, holy-pancake…this is the best.

Hell yeah she's coming back tomorrow.

[SIX]

"Watch your hands!" Matt yells to Kendra.

"Getting…heavy…hurry!" she yells back.

Matt walks backward into Kendra's apartment, carrying one end of her new sofa. "Almost there!" Kendra adjusts her grip on the other end.

They shuffle into the living room and begin to place the sofa down when suddenly, Matt's golden lab runs underneath. "Gracie! No!" he yells. Gracie barks then playfully runs into Kendra's kitchen.

"Three…two…one!" Kendra says, and they set it down. "I had no idea it was that heavy!"

Matt tumbles onto the plush, gray velvet sofa and stretches out. "Your taste for the fine things may kill me."

Mmmm, the fine things. Like his body on that sofa. And maybe her body next to his…wearing nothing but his t-shirt. Ohhh, and maybe a new pair of black patent, red-soled Louboutins…

She can't resist and piles on top of him, pressing her body tight against his. "This sofa is a perfect fit for two," she says, and begins to trail her lips across the side of his face until she reaches his ear. "You, and your dirty truck, saved me a ninety-nine dollar delivery fee. I owe you," she whispers.

He steals a kiss from her smiling lips. "I'll gladly take payment in kisses." He softly kisses her again. He's been stealing kisses from her all night, first nipping her ear while she was trying to check out at the furniture store, then giving her a head-spinning kiss after they loaded his truck.

"You weren't even going to see me until our second date tomorrow night," she whispers. "That was, until you rescued me from Wellington's Furniture tonight."

"Watching you blow your money was certainly a fun, spontaneous date," he says. "I can't believe you paid over a thousand dollars for this."

"What? It was on sale! I'm careful with my money. I wait until I can afford what I want and then," she digs her fingers into his side, "I snatch it!" They squirm together, giving each other playful kisses. Then Gracie whimpers from the kitchen. Matt lifts up his head to face her.

"Hold on, girl. I know you're hungry." He faces Kendra again. "Let me go down to my place and feed her dinner. I can come back up and maybe we can break in, I mean, sit together on this couch."

Her grin is so wide she can hardly kiss him again. But she does, with small kisses, again and again, higher to his ear. "Break in…sit…we can do both." She rolls off of him and extends a hand to help him up. He latches on and pulls himself off of the sofa.

"Davis is coming by in a bit," she says, "and he's bringing sandwiches. He knew you were helping me so he has one for you too. So, hurry back."

Matt heads toward the door and Gracie scampers alongside him. "Every time I come to your apartment, I get fed. I like this."

Kendra opens the door. Gracie runs out into the hallway and Matt follows. "I'll be back in about an hour," he says, eyes steaming. He leans in to give her a long, lingering kiss.

She shuts the door and lets out a sigh. *What a day.* Seeing him was the best part, although Nolan's blueberry pancake at Seven Spoons this morning is a close number two. Both of those were better than her day at the bank, where she did nothing right, according to Mrs. Danner. Kendra grabs a kitchen towel and walks over to her new furniture. She begins to wipe down the mahogany legs, dusty from Matt's truck, when she hears a knock at her door.

"Let me in or I'll eat it all," Davis yells.

She opens the door and he walks in, carrying a clear bag stuffed with foot-long sandwiches. "Dinner is served," he says, laying the bag on the counter.

"Perfect!" she says and grabs two bottled waters from the fridge. "Where's Susan?"

"She had to work late," he says, unwrapping his sandwich.

"Ahhh…putting in extra hours so she has time for your romantic, fall-in-New Hampshire honeymoon," Kendra says. "So, are you ready for the wedding Saturday?"

"Ready as I'll ever be!" he says. "It feels like I've waited forever for this moment…for the right person."

"You're only thirty-three years old! It's not like you're over the hill."

"I know…I just hope I've got it all right."

"You do! Are you having some doubts?"

"Susan just…I don't know…seems a little quiet. I hope she's not getting cold feet."

"Brides get nervous. That's normal, especially for a bride as popular as Susan. She'll be watched by so many people; she has so many friends!" Kendra opens her sandwich. "Speaking of friends, did…I mean…do you know…has Portia RSVP'd yet?"

"She did," Davis says. "And it was a no. She's not coming."

Thank you, Lord. "Good! I still have no idea why Susan and Portia are friends."

"Because Susan would be friends with a frog if she could." Davis looks at the extra, unopened sandwich. "Where's Matt?"

"He was just here…helping me bring up this beautiful, brand new sofa!" she says with a sweeping, dramatic gesture as if she were presenting the grand prize on a television game show.

Davis glances over. "That looks expensive. Let me guess: it was."

She drops her arm to her hip. "This girl gets what she wants. And as for Matt, he had to feed Gracie but said he'd be back in an hour."

"An hour? To feed a dog? Downstairs? This meatball sub will be mush!"

"He has other things to do, I guess. I don't care, as long as he comes back." She gives him a mischievous grin.

"You two have hit it off like gasoline and a match. Reminds me of when you were in middle school. Remember that kid, Bobby? He gave you his lunch and you called him your boyfriend by the end of the day."

"Yeah, I was excited."

"Then, high school. You offered a towel to that kid Eric on

the swim team and by the end of the week, he gives you his class ring."

"Why are you inventorying all of the guys I've ever liked?"

"Because I wanted to remind you of the one you last fell for. The blond, lacrosse-playing doctor that you were dating ONLY A WEEK AGO. It's not even been a week!"

She looks down to her sandwich and slowly picks out strands of shredded lettuce. "Don't think that I'm not thinking about Christopher. I am. All the time."

"You still haven't heard from him?"

"No. I don't think I will. At least, I probably shouldn't." She looks up. "But I've got to move on and I didn't think I'd run into someone as amazing as Matt this soon but…what am I supposed to do? Tell Matt to wait until I'm completely over Christopher?"

Davis begins to nod.

"No, stop," she says. "I'm not going to wait. I'm going to see where this thing between me and Matt goes."

Davis takes another bite of his sandwich. They eat in silence for a minute.

"Matt has a story too," he says. "There's an ex in town, claiming he has a temper…"

"Of course there is," she says, shaking her head. "Look what you just did a minute ago. You brought up all the guys I've liked in my lifetime and if you found them and asked them something bad about me, they'd have something to say. I'm not worried about Matt or his ex or any story. I'm moving on and he happens to be moving along with me."

They both take bites of their sandwich, slowly eating and continuing their conversation when there's a knock on the door.

She jumps up and glances in the mirror beside the door,

scrunching her straight brown hair. "You didn't tell me my makeup looked this bad!"

"What? I'm in charge of your beauty routine now? You look fine. For me. And him."

She wipes under her eye to remove some smudged mascara. She's always wished her brown eyes were blue, she's never liked her pudgy-looking nose and why can't she have naturally plump lips?

A second round of knocks sound at the door.

"Matt," she says, opening the door wide, "welcome back."

His smile leads him in and he gives her a kiss. "Hey, Davis," he says, giving Davis a bro-shake. "Oh man, thank you for picking this up for me." Matt unwraps the sandwich and quickly takes a huge bite.

"Dang, you are hungry," Kendra says. "And…dirty." She points to his boots and the dirt he's trailed in. "Did you walk Gracie in the woods or something?"

He looks down. "Oh gee, sorry." He picks up a napkin and wipes the bottoms of his boots. "I can take these off and sweep that up."

"Don't worry; it's all good."

"I'm a hungry, dirty mess."

That works for her.

"Speaking of dirty," Davis says, turning to Kendra, "remember not to wear heels to the wedding. I know how fashionable you are but we'll be in the grass at the winery for the ceremony part and I know that if your heels dig into the ground and get dirty, you'll blame me."

"I'm already ahead of you. I've got an adorable pair of wedges ready to roll," she says.

"Ugh," Matt grumbles, his mouth full with sandwich. He swallows and takes a sip of water. "Why did you guys have to pick the winery? I hate that place. Hate the owners more."

"Hate?" Kendra asks. "That's a strong word."

"Dislike with a passion, then, if that's better," he says.

"They're nice people. We got a good price too, since Susan is a city employee."

"And that's my problem," Matt says. "City taxpayers have bailed out the winery for years with this bogus tourism tax. And that's after the owners got a sweetheart tax deal from Tony Fletcher in the first place. They shouldn't need any more of our tax money."

"Why do they need a bail out anyway?" Kendra asks.

"Because they run the place poorly," Matt says. "I've been up there enough to know. Their management needs to be replaced with someone who knows the business…someone who knows how to run a business."

"Wait," Kendra says. "Let me guess. The guy who runs the winery is a friend of the mayor and a friend of your boss too."

"Exactly! They take our money for themselves and never use it for what they're supposed to."

Kendra looks down. And according to Susan, the mayor might be taking his hands places they're not supposed to be, either.

"You may have a point," Davis says. "When we went up there last weekend for the walkthrough, the place didn't look as good as it used to. Nothing was green; everything looked dry and brown."

"And you can't blame it on our drought. They have irrigation," Matt adds. "Someone around here needs to start asking questions and demanding answers."

Kendra steps toward Matt and places her hand on his shoulder. "You know so much about the history here, maybe you're the one to ask."

"It can't be me," he says. "I can't be chief if I get fired first."

"Then go to the press or someone else in town that can ask questions."

"I might," he says. "I just might."

Davis wads up his sandwich paper and shoots it like a basketball into the trash can. "End of the day for me. I'm going home. Glad you are getting settled, my friend."

She stands up and gives Davis a hug. "I can't wait until Saturday. I'm so happy for you."

He hugs her back and then heads for the door. "Hopefully my bride has gotten home."

"She should be by now," Matt says, his mouth full and his eyes on his sandwich.

The room quiets.

Matt looks up. "What? I saw her pull in a few minutes ago."

Davis cracks a smile. "For a second there I thought you two had something going on."

Matt dips his chin to his chest. "Maybe we *did* have something going on. But then Susan kicked me to the curb and claimed she loves you more."

Kendra swats Matt's shoulder and then steps to the door to face Davis. "Next time I see you, it'll be your wedding day."

He grimaces. "Don't be getting all weird. See you Saturday."

He leaves and Kendra shuts the door. Matt gets up from the table, his sandwich finished. He's close enough to Kendra to pull her into his arms. "The last thing I want to do on Saturday is go up to the stupid winery, but I'm doing it for two reasons."

"Two?" Kendra asks, adding a curious smile.

"One: Susan and I have been friends for a million years so there's no way I can miss this."

"And number two?"

"I hope to have the best-looking date on my arm. Will you go to the wedding with me?"

"I don't know…" she says, leaning closer to him. He settles his hands on her waist and gently squeezes her. She strokes his arms. "Another date? Are you worried we're moving too fast?"

"Not." He softly kisses her. "Worried." He kisses her again. "At." Another kiss. "All." He finishes his sentence with a long, slow kiss, pouring emotion into his lips while his hands squeeze her waist. Her muscles tremble and her heartbeat quickens. Their kisses become more urgent and he plunges his hands into her hair. They stagger and spin…kissing fast. Her brain scatters.

This. Him. Now.

He pushes her backward, toward the couch. He pulls her shirt over her head; she's already unbuttoned his jeans. He yanks off his boots; she helps him out of his jeans and he helps her out of hers and as he does she throws her bra across the room. They tumble in a fit of physical pleasure onto the sofa. Kiss-by-kiss and push-by-push, the man she met less than forty-eight hours ago becomes forever written into the most intimate story of her life.

Matt Livingston: her lover.

[SEVEN]

Kendra rushes into the kitchen, reaching for her car keys on the counter. Her sweeping grab pushes the keys and they crash to the floor. *Really? Now?* She's been running late since she woke up, exhausted after Matt left. And at 2 a.m. it was hard to see him go…

Carefully, she squats to pick her keys up. Now is not the time to rip her skirt! After eating so many delicious meals the past few days, her skirt feels tight. She grabs the keys, stands straight, smoothes out her navy suit and grabs her Louis Vuitton purse. *Leave. Seven Spoons. Get to work. Go.*

She flings open her apartment door and stops cold. A single yellow rose lies on her doormat. *No note?* Shoot: no note needed! She carefully squats again, picks it up and breathes in the sweet scent. *Oh, Matt.* Her eyes close, remembering him; them; and their incredible night of firsts. Who knew a tough guy like him could be so ticklish?

Then a memory slams into her and her eyes fly open. *Crap! Christopher?*

A heavy feeling fills her stomach. She quickly looks left, and then right. Christopher gave her a single yellow rose before! Twice!

Quickly she closes and locks her apartment door, puts the rose inside her purse, and dashes to her car. She backs out of her space and speeds away, looking in the rearview mirror to see if she's being followed.

The rising sun on Route 5 is smack in her line of sight again. It's hard to see straight, so she keeps her eyes on the side of the road, while trying to watch what—or who—may be behind her. Finally, she arrives in the Seven Spoons parking lot, pulls into a space and turns off her car.

Get a grip. If Christopher had found her apartment, he would have knocked. He wouldn't miss an opportunity to tell her again that she is wrong and he is right. He's a talker—and a charmer—and most people fall under his persuasive spell. She's seen it before. Whenever they dined out, he would mesmerize waitresses with flirtatious compliments, all for the sake of getting free drinks. He convinced his old college roommate to spend a weekend with them at the Outer Banks even though his old roommate hates the beach. She saw firsthand when he stood up to a Henrico County police officer who pulled him over for speeding. Somehow, his compliments and babbling got him only a warning instead of a costly ticket. He wouldn't waste his time now leaving a subtle message at her door with a flower. The rose must be from Matt.

She relaxes her shoulders, picks up her phone and begins to type a text.

Good morning. By any chance, did you leave

She stops typing. *What a stupid text.* She tries again.

Good morning. Can't stop thinking about last night.
You were full of surprises, like this morning

Stop. This is impossible. There's no good way to ask him if he left the rose, at least, not over text. And if she thanks him for it and he didn't leave it? She's told him she has an ex but she's sure not ready to tell him everything about Christopher yet.

She tosses her phone into her purse and opens her car door to head inside the restaurant. A quick glance over to the handicapped space confirms: old man Ellis is here. His old, silver, four-door sedan is sort of parked in the space again.

Soft, jingling bells tied to the door announce her arrival again, and the restaurant feels just as warm and fun as she remembered from yesterday.

Scruffy man is in the same spot, with his pancakes smothered in syrup and his toast spread with grape jelly. The music sounds different today. It's a seventies soundtrack! Scruffy man hums along to *Best of My Love.*

"Hello again," the same waitress says, looking less stressed than yesterday. "Just one?"

"Yeah, and I'll sit at the counter again if that's okay."

"Sure, honey. Help yourself!"

Kendra chooses the same barstool as yesterday, carefully sitting in a skirt that feels tighter by the minute. *No carbs today!* Chef Nolan works at the griddle, where hamburger buns holding cooked bacon are stacked to the left side and a massive slab of hash browns cooks on the right. Stainless-steel frying pans hang above the griddle, just past the wire that holds the customer orders. She catches him looking into the shiny back of one of the frying pans. He's looking at her. He turns around.

"Hello again," he says, his dimpled smile stretching. "Come back to watch my buns?"

Her gaze flicks up and then back down. "I'm never going to live that down, am I?"

"Never." He slides a menu toward her. "Pancake again?"

She slumps. "Got anything healthier? Like an omelet, no cheese and some veggies?"

His expression softens, as if he can read her mind. "Egg-white?"

"Oh, even better!"

He's already turned around, taking one of the fry pans off of the rack and cracking open some eggs, carefully removing the yokes. He places the frying pan on the griddle.

"So, why don't you cook the eggs on the griddle with everything else?" Kendra asks, fascinated with how quickly he works and how unique his cooking methods are.

He turns slightly toward her. "Egg-white people usually don't want the bacon-fat taste, so I use a separate pan."

Of course. "You're good at this, aren't you?"

He turns over the cooking eggs with a spatula. "A man can't be a man unless he knows how to use a frying pan." He glances over his shoulder, flashing his smile.

God, his dimples are hot.

The waitress brushes her shoulder, leaning closer. "I see Nolan's got your attention, and your order," she says with a flat look and narrow eyes. "Coffee with that?" Her tart voice seems to draw a line.

Oh crap. No! Not here to steal your boyfriend! "Coffee would be great, thank you," Kendra says. The waitress begins to turn away and Kendra stops her. "I'm Kendra. I didn't get to meet you yesterday. It seemed crazy in here."

"Yeah, it was nuts," she says, turning away.

So much for trying to get to know her.

While Nolan stays busy adding veggies to her omelet, she turns to see the two older guys in the corner booth, who are pointing to each other and laughing just like they did yesterday. One of them catches her eye and he waves her over. "Okay, you over there, you can be the final vote," he says.

"Vote for what?" Kendra asks, sliding off of her stool and approaching their booth.

"This is serious stuff," the man says, pushing up a pair of glasses that have slipped down the bridge of his nose.

The other man turns to face her. "Don't listen to anything my brother says."

"Brothers?" Kendra asks.

"Unfortunately for me," he says.

She sticks out her hand. "I'm Kendra, with a brother myself."

The man with the glasses shakes her hand. "Marvin, and that's my brother Glen."

Glen smiles smugly, looking confident even while wearing a pink polo shirt. His face wears fewer wrinkles; his cheeks fuller than his brother's. He must be the younger one.

"So what am I voting for?" Kendra asks.

The waitress interrupts them, leaning in to put a plate of scrambled eggs in front of Marvin, and a plate with a pancake in front of Glen. "Behave with the new people you guys, would ya?" she says and then walks away.

"Come on, Gina! I never have and I never will!" Marvin yells back to her.

Kendra watches Gina walk away. So that's her name!

Marvin tugs Kendra's arm. "Distinguished men do not wear pink. Am I correct?"

Glen sits up straight, chest out and raises the collar on his pink polo.

"He's in pink," Kendra says, pointing her thumb to Glen. "Am I voting on whether he looks distinguished, if he's a man, or if he looks good in pink?"

"Oh I know I look good in anything," Glen says, chin up. "My brother has a problem with pink."

Kendra smiles. "I love a man in pink."

"See!" Glen says, slapping his hands on the table.

"But…" Kendra says. "I don't know you, so you might not be distinguished."

"Ha!" Marvin says, slapping *his* hands on the table.

The man in the next booth interrupts them. "What's a five-letter word for a corrupting or debilitating influence that begins with a u?" he says, looking up from his crossword puzzle.

"U, Glen," Marvin says, pointing to Glen.

"U, Marv," Glen says, pointing to Marvin.

"Ulcer," Kendra says.

The man looks down and writes on his puzzle. "Ulcer! That's it!"

"Glad we could help you again, Jay," Glen says, smug.

"She's beautiful and smart," says old man Ellis, who has just stood up from his table, his breakfast finished. He positions his walker and grips the handles, taking a frail and shaky step forward. Kendra reaches to help him, but he waves her off. "I'm fine," he says, shuffling forward. He looks even paler than yesterday.

"You should have stayed at home, buddy. You can't even walk," Marvin says.

Old man Ellis pauses. "If I stop, then it's all over for me," he says, attempting a joke.

"I could have brought you breakfast," Glen says.

Kendra chimes in. "I would have brought you breakfast too!"

"At my age, there's a problem every day. This is nothing," Ellis says.

Kendra follows him to open the door. Right as they approach it, Nolan leans over the counter. "Ellis, I'm taking you to the doctor next week," he calls out. "And if you fuss, I'll put prunes in your pancake."

"Awww…" Ellis says. "Very, very funny."

Kendra opens the door and Ellis shuffles out, making his way to his car. She takes her seat again on the barstool, her omelet waiting on a plate. Nolan faces her, but like yesterday he's watching Ellis get into his car.

"He's usually as healthy as a horse," Nolan says. "Something isn't right…"

[EIGHT]

Kendra clutches Matt's arm as they walk down a gravel pathway lined with burnt-orange and golden-yellow mums. White candles in mason jars light up the dusk air and a small band has begun playing celebratory music.

Mr. and Mrs. Davis Perkins pose for post-ceremony photographs while Kendra, Matt and the rest of the guests make their way from the outdoor ceremony down to the winery tavern for the reception.

Kendra squeezes Matt's arm and snuggles closer to him. Her off-the-shoulder, burgundy lace dress is no match for the falling temperature. Right now, she's content absorbing Matt's warmth, even though he's seemed stiff all evening.

"What would you be doing now, here, at this wedding, if you hadn't met me a week ago?" she asks.

He grips her arm and squeezes. "I'd be having a worse time than I already am," he grumbles. "Don't take that the wrong way; this is no fault of yours, of course."

Of course.

"I would have been here anyway. Do you think we would have noticed each other?" she asks.

"Hell yeah, I would have noticed you. Especially your smile and the way your hair looks so soft." He nuzzles his mouth closer to her ear. "And your dress...definitely would've had my eyes on that lace, trying to watch your skin peek through it."

She giggles softly. *Finally, he's softening up!* "Really?"

"Oh really. Seriously though, if you weren't here, I would have already left by now."

And back to grumpy.

They approach the old, wooden tavern—a small restaurant used by the winery for events and tastings. They follow the other guests inside, where dark-stained wine barrels serve as table bases and bows tied with sheer orange ribbon are everywhere. On the center of each table are white, tapered candles in empty wine bottles, with wax dripping down the bottle sides. Kendra and Matt stand in a corner, looking around. A bar has just opened up across the room, and a long line quickly forms. Maybe a stiff drink will loosen him up again.

"Let's get a drink," she says.

He shakes his head, fidgeting.

"You really don't like this winery and the people who run it, do you?"

He reaches for her shoulders, gently squeezing them and then pulling her closer. "I don't. I don't like people who get away with things. It's not fair."

"You need proof," Kendra says. "You need to figure out how to prove once and for all that these people are stealing taxpayer money. Otherwise, this theory you have will eat the happiness out of your life."

He moves his hands down her arms to hold her hands. "You are the happiness in my life right now. You are the only person who listens to me. Everyone else thinks I should shut up and mind my own business. It makes me mad when people try to shut me down."

She shakes her head. "No, no…you shouldn't give up. You have a pretty good hunch something is happening. You need to get proof, or you need to drop it."

Matt nods to the left. "See? Over there? Daisy and Rip; Betty and Tony. The power couples in town. They make more money than I'll ever see. And how can that be? How can they take long vacations, live in big houses and buy new things?"

She glances their way. God only knows what, and how much, perfume The Betty is wearing tonight. "Maybe their families always had money."

"They didn't. I know," he says. The sound of laughter rises up from their table and his eyes tighten. "Here's another example of what is wrong around here. A few months ago we had a fundraising drive to collect money to replace a playground that had burned down. Then a few months later, the Fletchers' house suddenly got a sunroom expansion. Maybe he used his own money, but you know what? That playground still hasn't been fixed. That money is in some city account. Rip tells us there's not enough money yet to finish the playground. But we collected several thousand dollars. How much does it cost to build a swing set or a slide or something?"

Suddenly a tall, black-haired man with a thick mustache enters the room and everyone seems to turn and acknowledge his presence.

"Who's that?" Kendra asks.

"The winery owner, James Landry," Matt whispers. "He's as crooked as they come. I mean, look at this place." He gestures around the tavern. The wood floor is worn bare in the high traf‑fic areas, old lighting fixtures make the room dim, plus every‑thing smells musty. "They haven't improved this joint in years, but every year, we pay more for a tourism tax that they get their money from."

"A tourism tax? In Cory City? For…this?"

Matt nods, still watching James Landry make his entrance.

Kendra watches James too and leans closer to Matt. "If he has a good budget, I wonder why he's not even watering outside. Davis was right: the vines and all of his landscaping looked so dry."

"His vines are his paycheck, so you'd think he'd want to take care of them. But no. He's probably going to blame it on a drought or faulty irrigation and then file a big insurance claim and get more money." Matt clears his throat and avoids eye contact with the man. Over on the other side of the room, voices erupt in jolly hellos as the winery owner greets the mayor, the fire chief and their wives.

"So cozy," Kendra says, watching their air kisses and shoul‑der hugs. She faces Matt, who is also watching them. His nostrils flare and a vein throbs in his neck. *Holy shit.* "Hey," she says, trying to change his focus.

Then his phone rings. He quickly pulls it out and answers curtly, "This is Matt."

He listens, going still, and all she wants to do is hug him right now. He's so tense! So pissed! If she could wrap him in her arms, maybe slip her fingers under his shirt and find that spot on his waist she found the night they first made love. He giggled—adorably giggled—when she stroked him there. She wants soft, giggly Matt back!

"Be there in a minute," he barks, and then hangs up.

Her shoulders slump. "What happened?"

He glances over her head, looking to the corner where Tony and Rip are standing. "You're not going to believe this: another busted hydrant over on Travis." He looks back into her eyes. "I'm so sorry, but I've got to go."

"Okay, we can go."

"No…you should stay. Stay and have fun. Say hello to Susan and Davis for me. Is there anyone here who can drive you home?"

Kendra glances around and sees a co worker, head teller Cindy. "I'll ask Cindy. I'm sure she could give me a ride."

He heads toward the door and she walks faster just to keep up with him. The least she can do is walk with him to his truck. They rush away from the tavern, bolting to the parking lot. He reaches his truck and turns to face her, his expression urgent and worried. "I'm sorry I have to go."

She grabs his head and pulls him to her for a kiss. Her lips try to soften him, to comfort him.

He pulls back, looking at her with uneasy eyes. *He's sad? Mad? Scared?* A lump in her throat makes it hard for her to swallow.

"I'll call you later," he says, getting into his truck.

"Please be safe. I'm getting worried about you."

He nods.

She stands, confused, watching him drive away. His sense of right and wrong is so strong but his deep passion to fix everything makes this so…complicated. Will this be the new normal dating a fireman? An aching heart and sick stomach every time he responds to an emergency?

Matt's taillights disappear just as Kendra hears wild cheers and applause from the tavern. Davis and Susan must have made their grand reception entrance.

She slowly begins the walk back, the lump in her throat now making her mouth feel dry. Breezy, cool air once again sends shivers down her body, yet with every step closer to the tavern, she's getting warmer. Hotter. Her heart pounds with intention and irritation pulses through her veins. She passes a planter of bushes. All of the leaves look brown and crispy from the lack of water. *These people; such selfish crooks. And the mayor with his filthy, hot hands.* Since she's the new girl in town, what the hell does she have to lose? Maybe it's time for her to meet these people, ask some questions and dig deeper to find answers for Matt.

She plows through the tavern door to find the reception in high gear. Davis and Susan must have completed their first dance because now they're dancing with the crowd, their hands in the air, enjoying the fast beat of the music. Other guests walk past with plates full of food, and from all of the tables with chairs tipped forward in "reserved" positions and from those already seated, it looks like most everyone has claimed a spot at a table. Cindy and her husband happen to pass by.

"Hey, Kendra!" Cindy says. Her husband's eyes are glued to his plate, piled high with brisket, beans and cornbread.

Kendra hugs her. "Hey, there. My date had to leave. Any chance you can give me a ride home?"

"Of course!" Cindy says. "Just tell us when you're ready to go!" They move past her and Kendra looks across the room to the table of mischief. Tony and Betty, Rip and Daisy and the winery guy James are all seated together. Since she's met The

Betty once, why not go up and introduce herself again?

Eyes on their table, Kendra makes her way across the room when someone taps her shoulder. She turns around.

"I'm trapped!" Davis yells over the music, holding up his left hand and his brand new wedding ring. His smile bursts with joy. *What a goof.*

"Finally!" Kendra yells, opening her arms for a hug. Davis squeezes her tight, high on love and on top of the world.

He pulls back. "Can you believe a beautiful girl thought I was worth it?"

"I think she's nuts but I guess she landed a good man," Kendra says, poking him in the chest.

Susan runs up behind him, her blushing face filled with joy, her veil headpiece tilted to one side. She keeps robustly hugging every guest as if they were her favorite teddy bear. No wonder her veil's been tugged a bit. She opens her arms and gives Kendra a teddy bear hug. They step away from each other.

"You look stunning," Kendra says.

Davis wraps his arm around Susan. "Hey? I'm not cute?" he asks.

Kendra smiles. "You're alright."

"Where's Matt?" Susan asks, looking around.

"He had an emergency and left. He asked me to send his love."

Susan's blushing face goes cold. She moves out of Davis's hold. "Where'd he go?"

"Another bursting hydrant on Travis. He wasn't very happy about it."

"What the hell is happening over there?" Davis asks.

Susan's shoulders deflate and her smile falls away. Then a

young woman wearing a tight, bright blue dress approaches her. "Hey, Susan! Congratulations!" she says. Susan straightens and perks up, greeting her friend with a squeal and another big teddy bear hug, jumping right back into the role of blushing bride. Davis turns to meet the girl and Kendra slips away.

Back to her mission.

She passes the bar. *Get a drink in hand as a prop?* That would look casual. *No.* Go in with two open hands. That way she can give hearty fake handshakes and hugs.

Kendra approaches the crooked-people table just as The Betty notices her.

"Well hello!" Betty calls out from her seat. "You're Louise's new assistant manager, right?"

Kendra flashes a toothpaste commercial smile. "Yes! Hello, Mrs. Fletcher!" She sucks in a breath, holds it, steps next to Betty's seat and sticks out her hand. "Kendra."

Betty shakes her hand. "Of course! Such a lovely girl and name."

Kendra exhales. Her next breath in makes her nose sting. *Shit, woman.* The Betty smells like she applied every perfume sample from the department store. No, not the department store. Those are high-end perfumes. This lady hit the dime store and sampled every brand.

Betty smiles with pride. "Everyone…I met Kendra the other day at the bank. She's new in town."

Mayor Tony Fletcher stands. "Welcome to Cory City." He extends his hand in a warm handshake while his eyes lower to look at her chest.

Creep. Kendra squeezes his hand back. "Thank you."

"Meet my friends," Betty says.

The mayor still has Kendra's hand and she gently shakes him off. If she could run to the bathroom and wash it without making a scene, she would.

"Rip Fletcher," Rip says, standing to shake her hand. Rip is a slender, older man with years of life creased into his face, but his smile looks inviting and comfortable, like a grandfather. "This is my wife, Daisy."

Daisy turns from her seat and affectionately shakes Kendra's hand. "It's lovely to see and meet new, younger people moving to this town."

Kendra nods. *Odd. Like, nicely odd.*

Daisy warmly touches Kendra's arm. "We need younger people like you to bring life to this old place."

Kendra notices an empty bottle of wine, and an empty wine glass, in front of Daisy's plate. *Sweet.* A juiced-up, crooked spouse will certainly spill information, if Kendra can ask the right questions. And her first question to Daisy might be why she gave The Betty five grand. Except in the end that question might get her fired.

Daisy looks around the table. "We've all been here too long. Isn't it nice to see some fresh faces?" Everyone nods.

Rip raises his glass to toast the air. "Hear, hear!"

Really? Kendra smiles. "So, would you like to just give me the keys to the city now?"

Mayor Fletcher stands up and digs into his pocket to pull out his keys. He holds them up. "I've been waiting for someone to come along and take these from me!"

Everyone laughs.

"We're happy you're here, Kendra," Betty says. "If you ever need anything from any of us, please just ask."

Kendra nods, standing in an awkward state of delusion. Either she's getting hosed with their nice guy act, or these are really normal people. Except for the mayor and his dirty eyes.

Mustache man James approaches the table, with a full glass of red wine.

"Have you met Kendra?" Daisy asks.

"No, hello," he says, shaking Kendra's hand. But he never tells her his name. Guess he thinks he's so popular he doesn't need to introduce himself.

"You run this winery, right?" Kendra asks.

"I do! Is this your first time here?" he asks, leaning in.

"It is! It's so beautiful, except I couldn't help but notice everything looks so dry…"

Bite the bait! Answer that, cheap man!

He nods. "You've noticed, and I apologize for that. We were hoping to have our problem fixed before we hosted Susan's wedding." He stands taller. "Our vineyard manager is stumped. Our irrigation hasn't changed, yet our vines and landscaping keep turning brown. I asked a viticulturist from one of the state universities to come in next week to help us."

Bet that costs a lot. "Very interesting. I just assumed you may be having a problem with watering."

He sighs heavily. "Oh, no. These vines are like my children. This winery is my family! Believe me, we're trying our best to take care of them. Would you like to come back for a tour sometime?"

To check your irrigation system settings? "Maybe, that would be nice."

Daisy waves from her seat. "I'll join you if you don't have anyone to go with."

Kendra looks at Daisy's soft eyes and inviting expression. Maybe Daisy wants to come along so she can drink more wine. Or, maybe she's being genuinely kind. Could they be masters of deception? Or are Matt and Susan way off the mark?

The music stops and everyone's attention turns to the dance floor, where single ladies are gathering for the bouquet toss— her least favorite part of any wedding. *Hide. Fast!* "Nice to meet you all," Kendra says, politely nodding and quickly stepping away. There's a good chance she'd get dragged onto the dance floor by The Betty or Daisy or worse: the mayor.

Kendra retreats to the back of the room. Most people are standing to watch, so hiding behind them is a safe bet. And she needs to stay hidden. If Davis notices she's not out there, he'll hunt her down and force her out.

Susan's face beams with joy as she kisses her bouquet and then turns her back on the ladies. "Three! Two! One!" she yells, throwing her bouquet in the air.

Hands frantically reach up but the bouquet seems to magically float to the side, to a well-dressed woman standing on the edge of the crowd. She effortlessly reaches one hand up and snatches the bouquet.

Women scream in delight but none as loud as Susan. "Yes!" Susan squeals, running to the woman. They embrace and spin in a circle and with each spin, Kendra slowly recognizes what the woman is wearing.

Black Prada pumps.

St. John suit; evening collection.

David Yurman bracelets, classic cuff—a couple of them.

Her short, black hair is professionally styled in a well-done wedge haircut.

Suddenly, Kendra can't breathe.

Shit! Portia Randall!

She wasn't supposed to come! *Not supposed to be here!*

Her first instinct: run. She's not ready to face Christopher's bitchy, big sis. Not here. *Not now!* Find Cindy and get the hell out of here.

She moves quickly, darting around people. *Find…Cindy!*

Sounds in the room seem to mute and everyone she's passing looks like a blur. This isn't that big of a room! Why can't she find her? *Where the hell is Cindy?*

She turns a corner, near the table where she last saw Cindy and her husband, when someone cups her elbow. *Thank God!* She spins to face Cindy.

Her legs stiffen and her breath hitches, her body suddenly frozen in fear.

"Going somewhere?" asks Christopher Randall.

[NINE]

Kendra cannot breathe…move…swallow…think.

"Looks like you're running away," Christopher says. "Again."

She clutches her chest. An icy chill rushes down her legs. "What are you doing here?"

Their eyes lock and for a long moment, they simply stare. His eyes sizzle; her eyes are still in shock. Finally, his lips part. "Portia wanted to come at the last minute, so I drove her. I was hoping you would be here."

Her arms loosen, dropping to her sides. She feels small and gulps down what feels like marbles. "We can't do this here."

He nods. His thick blond hair is stylishly swept to the side. Of course he wore his windowpane gray Tom Ford suit, the one she helped him pick out. That gray suit and his cobalt blue tie are making his sad, blue eyes glow. The soft lines of his nose trace down to his lips. *Those lips.* They used to be hers. *He* used to be hers. She's shrinking by the second.

"I know you don't agree with what I did…" he says.

"Stop. No. This is way bigger than me and my feelings." She leans closer. "You could get arrested."

He leans in. "And now you could too."

"You *should* be arrested."

"You should have minded your own business. What's with you, anyway? Digging in to other people's business to…what? Help? You ruined us because of it."

Her blood pressure spikes. She stands taller.

"*I* ruined us? I can't live a lie. People could get killed, Christopher. This isn't some small crime. You can play it down, but your day is going to come."

"We have a deal."

"And we still do…"

They stand close enough to feel each other's breath. Music plays and people pass by, unaware of their swirling drama. She presses even closer, to whisper in his ear. "We do still have a deal…but it makes me disgusted with how you're using our love against me."

He presses his lips against her ear. "You're the greatest love I've ever known. I was ready to give you everything. All I asked for was loyalty, trust and belief."

She grits her teeth and then puts her lips back on his ear. "And I gave you loyalty. I gave you everything. All of me. And it was the mistake of my life to let you record me doing it."

"I never want that video to get out but I swear, Kendra, I swear, I will do anything I have to do to protect myself."

She stays pressed to his ear. "Erase the tape and turn yourself in."

She feels his exhale on her ear. "Come back to me and I will."

She jolts backward. "No way. No way you will. Been there, done that." She takes another step away. "No, Christopher. We're done."

His eyes look glazed and empty, his head leaning to one side. "Kendee, oh baby…"

Kendee. Her nickname and the last word he'd gently whisper before they'd finish making love. Her soul still burns for this man. For six glorious months they started building a life together. His career as a doctor seemed so promising; anything she wanted he gave her. They talked about their dream house, filled one day with children. Until…

She shakes her head. *Matt.* Why couldn't he still be here?

"I can't," she says.

A woman's voice loudly interrupts them. "Hey, Kendra! We're ready to leave now. Are you good to go?" says Cindy, teetering a bit, an empty wine glass in her hand.

Kendra turns to Cindy. "Yes. Now. Good to go."

"Okay! My husband went to pull the car around. Meet us outside!" she exclaims and begins dancing her way toward the door.

Kendra faces Christopher. She aches looking at him. But she can't live a life of lies.

"I loved you, Christopher. Don't blame me for your bad choices."

He swallows hard.

"But," she says, "if you ever loved me, if you still love me… erase that damn tape."

His chin rises. "I do still love you…"

His lips stop moving and the silence hangs heavy in the air. He's not saying more! He's not promising to get rid of it!

Damn it! Damn him!

Done.

She turns to walk away, to get away from him, to forget this ever happened, to try to move on. *Just get out of here.* She knows she needs to say goodbye to Susan and Davis. She wanted to see their grand sparkler exit, especially after tying ribbons on half of those fricken sparklers! But now the exit door is in sight. Cindy's car will be waiting. She's got to get the hell away from Christopher!

"Slow down, sister," a woman's voice says.

Portia Randall plants herself squarely in front of her.

Kendra stops, her body tense. "I'm not your sister."

"And to think you might have been, that is, before you broke my brother's heart," Portia says. Her flaming red lipstick looks as angry as her expression. She's breathtaking up close, so pulled together and visually perfect. "I knew from the moment I met you that you couldn't be trusted. And I was right. You ditched my brother and I'm warning you, if you ever, *ever*, breathe a word about what my brother and I have done, you will answer to me."

Kendra's pulse surges. She swats Portia away.

"No, Portia. I will answer to a judge. And I have a better shot of getting off than you do, because you should be in jail with him." She begins to walk around her.

Portia grabs her elbow. "Bitch."

Kendra pulls in a fighting breath and fists her hands. *Hit her where it hurts. And hit her hard.* She leans closer. "Your caviar shimmer St. John suit is sooo last season."

Portia drops her hand and Kendra rushes out the door.

[TEN]

Kendra sits alone at the Seven Spoons counter, wearing jeans and a sweatshirt with a ripped seam on the side, staring at her half-empty coffee cup. Usually, sitting here on her favorite stool makes her happy. Instead, she's nursing a hangover. And not an alcohol-induced one.

Truth and guilt are making her sick. A hammer swings over her head, waiting to drop and ruin her. Whenever Christopher chooses, her sex tape could go public. She squeezes her eyes closed. The wig, the costume, the dirty little performance of her life…all done for his amusement. *What an idiot she was.* He could blackmail her for the rest of her life.

She sips her coffee, shyly glancing over to Marvin and Glen. They're in their usual corner booth, laughing like they always do. Glen is showing Marvin some video from his phone. What if they see the tape someday? Her family? Or the mayor? Or, God forbid, Mrs. Danner? She'd have to run away again, to another town, and start all over.

It's a little after 7 a.m. on a Sunday morning, not exactly the breakfast rush hour on a weekend, but she wouldn't mind some company on this long line of barstools. Maybe if someone else was sitting here too she might feel less exposed and abandoned. She looks down to her phone to reread Matt's texts.

Saturday 12:15 am
Just got home and don't want to wake you. I'm sorry I had to leave. All is well. I am fine. Take you to breakfast tomorrow?

Having breakfast together was a perfect idea. Until 6:15 a.m.

Hey, got a call I need to help with. Raincheck on breakfast but I owe you something. Dinner?

She clicks off her phone. Hopefully he's safe, but she's doubtful that dinner will happen.

Nolan slides a plate with a banana granola pancake in front of her. He's put sliced bananas in the middle and laid out the granola in lines to look like the sun.

"I know you wanted a veggie omelet but it's easier for me to cheer you up with this," he says.

She lays a hand over her heart. "This is one of the nicest things anyone has done for me in a while." His food art looks delicious. *Screw healthy; she's going in.* Fork in hand, she takes a bite. Nolan still faces her, elbows on the counter, head in his hands.

"You had a bad night?" he asks.

She swallows and looks up at him. "The worst."

"I saw you a couple of times at the reception but could never catch your eye to say hi."

"You were there?"

"All afternoon and evening. We catered it. Are you telling

me you didn't eat my brisket?" He straightens and puts his hands on his hips.

She curls her shoulders. "I didn't eat anything at all last night."

"Oh. If we had any leftovers, I'd make you an after-the-fact to-go plate." He starts wiping off the counter. "I saw you were with Matt Livingston."

"You know Matt?"

He opens his mouth to say something, then closes it and looks away. "Yeah. I know him. He's been in here before. Not many people order the four-meat omelet but when he comes in, he always does."

Kendra glances down. One day, she'll come in here with Matt too. One day.

Nolan turns to his griddle, moves around some bacon and then turns back to her. "Anything I can help you with?" His expression is soft, his smile burns warm. This guy always seems happy. But unless he knows a good lawyer, and maybe a cyber-security expert who can remotely scrub a raunchy video from a computer, he probably can't help.

"You've made mistakes, right?" she asks. "I mean, at some point you have to mess up the cheese in someone's omelet or burn a slice of toast, right?"

"All the time."

"How do you stay so happy and positive when you mess up?"

"Because I know there's more to life than being sad about burnt toast."

"What if your mistake is bigger than a slice of toast?"

He straightens, flips some hash browns and then faces her.

"Life is burnt toast. You know, I didn't get great grades in high school so I missed my shot at going to a good culinary school. Instead of getting sad, I figured out a way around it. I focus on my goal—that's what keeps me happy and positive."

Kendra sits up straight, on the edge of her barstool. "What's your goal?"

"To be a chef at my own restaurant. Someplace where I can create food that makes people happy. I mean, I make a lot of new dishes here at Seven Spoons, but one day I want my own place."

"How old are you anyway?"

"Such a personal question!" He twists his shoulders, acting shy. "I'm twenty-seven."

"Wow! I'm twenty-six! I thought you were younger than me."

"It must be my good-looking buns."

She shakes her head. The buns joke will haunt her forever.

He peels off aluminum foil from a loaf of bread and cuts off a slice. "Here, try this."

"A new recipe?" Kendra says, reaching for the slice and taking a bite.

"Yeah, honey bread. I've been tweaking it but finally found the missing ingredient to make it perfect."

"Mmmm," Kendra says. "Sweet and light, like a sweet bread. I've never tasted anything like this before." He hands her another sample and when she reaches for it their hands briefly touch, just as Gina walks up to the counter.

Gina pushes a paper with a new order toward Nolan. "Here, baby."

He snatches the paper. "Gotcha, my love."

Kendra plasters on a big smile and tries to catch Gina's eye, but instead Gina gives her a cold glare, then turns and walks away. *Oh boy.* She didn't mean to flirt with Nolan, even though a guy like him would be totally fun to flirt with. She needs to get to know Gina better and reassure her that she's not here to take her man. As soon as Matt has a morning free and they can come in together, that might help.

Kendra finishes her honey bread sample, licking her fingers for every last sweet taste and turns back to watch Nolan. He begins to crack eggs, separating the yokes from the egg whites, and then grabs a shiny stainless-steel frying pan. "Ah…I see what you're doing," she says, remembering how he never cooks egg whites on the griddle but in a frying pan. "No man can be a man unless he knows how to use a frying pan."

"Oh yeah, baby!" he says, pouring the eggs into the pan.

She takes another bite of her pancake. *So good.* But how sad is it that she never tasted Nolan's brisket last night? Or said goodbye to Susan and Davis. Just thinking about last night again makes her throat feel thick.

Scruffy man behind her has been humming—and occasionally blurting out some words—to *Heard It Through The Grapevine.* "Hey, Nolan," he hollers.

Nolan turns. "Yes, my man Bobby?"

"What do we need to take up to the hospital today?"

Kendra tilts her head. *Hospital?*

"I've got a batch of chicken noodle soup going and I think he'll like this new honey bread I made."

"He?" Kendra asks.

Nolan wipes his hands on his apron, turning to give her his full attention. "Yeah. On my way to the winery yesterday, I stopped by old man Ellis's house. He doesn't live far from there. Anyway, he was having a hard time breathing, so I took him to the hospital."

Now Kendra feels like she's having a hard time breathing too. "Is he okay?"

"He was holding his own when I was up there," Bobby says from behind her. "They kept him overnight. But once he sees our faces today, I'm sure he'll feel better."

Marvin chimes in from his corner booth. "I was there last night and saw firsthand: he felt better once Bobby left."

"Well, I sometimes can have that effect on people," Bobby says, and begins humming again as he spreads jelly on his toast.

Kendra turns to Nolan. "I'll come up with you guys. What time are you going?" She feels unusually nervous and takes a deep breath to try to calm her suddenly racing heart.

Glen and Marvin have gotten up from their booth and are now heading for the exit. "We're meeting here at noon, right? Glad you're coming too! " Marvin says, patting Kendra on the back.

Damn! His pat makes her head spin. *What's wrong?* She wobbles on her stool.

Nolan turns from his griddle and lets out a gasp. He lurches over the counter, so far that his chest presses on her plate. "Kendra?" He reaches for her face. "Are you okay?"

His words blur...she floats backwards...into someone's arms. Nolan jumps over the counter and grabs her head. "Kendra!"

And that's the last blurry word she hears.

[ELEVEN]

An irritating beeping sound makes Kendra stir. She shakes off a chill and blinks open her eyes.

Nolan sits beside her, in her hospital bed, holding her hand. He looks her over and wrinkles his brow.

"Well, at least you were able to take a five-minute nap." He smiles, but it doesn't reach his eyes.

Her eyes flutter into focus, looking around her curtained space in the emergency room. The beeping machine returns to making quieter sounds. "That alarm is getting old. How much longer do you think I'll be here?"

"I know. It's almost lunchtime. Hopefully you won't be in here much longer. I've dispatched the best detectives in town to find out that answer."

Suddenly, someone pushes the curtain open. Marvin and Glen step inside wearing goofy smiles. "Hey! You woke up!" Marvin says.

Glen looks at Marvin. "Of course she woke up. How's she supposed to leave if she's asleep?"

"Find anyone to discharge her yet?" Nolan asks.

Marvin crosses his arms. "It's hard to find anyone who

works here, period. This place is a mess. There's only one doctor here!"

Glen nods. "You'd think since the waiting room is packed, they'd want you—and us—gone."

"This is ridiculous. I'm not going to pass out again. I should free up this bed for someone who needs it," Kendra says, even though she feels groggy and has a headache.

Nolan shrugs. "You can't leave yet, so you might as well rest now." He's still holding her hand.

"Look at that, Kendra," Glen says, pointing at their hands. "The guy who tried to kill you is trying to take care of you."

Kendra smiles and squeezes Nolan's hand. "You'll do anything to cover up my attempted murder, huh?"

Nolan's shoulders shrink. "Well, if everyone with food allergies would kindly tell me about their allergies, I'd have a shot at keeping them alive."

She smirks. "I know…I know."

Glen nods. "Speaking of keeping people alive, it's a good thing we brought Ellis your soup. Who knows when they'll get around to serving lunch."

Kendra tries to sit up but Nolan gestures for her to lie down. "How's he doing?" she asks.

"They can't figure out why his blood pressure is high," Marvin says.

Nolan's phone vibrates. He lets go of Kendra's hand to read a text. "It's Gina, asking how you're doing."

"Wow," Kendra says. "How incredibly sweet."

"She took over for me when we rushed you to the hospital. She's one of a kind," Nolan says, quickly texting her back and then tucking his phone in his back pocket. He gives her hand a squeeze. This is the first time she's ever seen him without his navy baseball cap. His thick, wavy, jet-black hair looks amazingly undone. His sideburns edge down his cheeks and even his brown eyes seem to smile. Inside and out, there's nothing unattractive about this man. Gina is one lucky girl.

"You and Gina make the cutest couple," she says, smiling.

"What?" Nolan asks, his voice an octave higher.

"Couple?" Marvin blurts.

Glen smirks. "Hey, let's get that incestuous rumor started in this small town."

Incestuous?

"Wait. Gina's your…"

"Sister," Nolan says.

Kendra rolls her eyes. "She's so adorable and you're so adorable and you call each other baby and love so I just thought you two adorable people would be…oh I can't believe I thought that!"

"I'm adorable?" Nolan says, sitting up straight. "You guys hear that?"

"She's medicated. She didn't mean it," Glen says.

Marvin puffs out his chest. "Just remember, when Kendra was falling, who did she fall into? Me. My arms…"

The curtain sweeps open and a nurse quickly walks in. "Okay, Ms. King, just a few things to sign and you're on your way."

Nolan lets go of Kendra's hand, gets off of the bed and steps away. Kendra sits up and gently swings her legs off the bed, still wearing the same jeans and sweatshirt she wore when she stepped into Seven Spoons this morning. She grabs the clipboard.

Marvin leans down to see the paperwork Kendra is signing.

"Is there a complete release of all charges against the killer chef?"

Glen leans down too. "Some affidavit saying he must disclose all ingredients before serving food to people?"

Nolan's eyes lower. "I'm gonna put crushed lima beans into your next omelets, guys. There, I just told you."

The nurse seems too rushed to be amused. "You're lucky, Ms. King, that Mr. Ford here had an epinephrine auto injector at the restaurant for anaphylactic reactions. You might be staying overnight if he hadn't, or worse."

Kendra signs the papers and looks up at Nolan. "He saved me. Well, first he poisoned me but then he saved me."

Nolan smiles a half-smile.

The nurse shuffles through the papers and then glances at Nolan. "That was fast detective work on your part, Mr. Ford. How did you realize so quickly that she was having a sesame seed reaction?"

"I guessed it had to be from my bread she sampled," he says. "I knew it wasn't peanut or wheat because I hadn't used those and she's eaten my pancakes before and had no issues. Then I remembered I had used a sesame seed oil in the bread. Evidently, it was too cheap of an oil because it affected her."

"What does being cheap have to do with it?" Marvin asks.

"It's the protein that causes a food allergy and good oils will burn that protein off. Reactions are more likely to happen when you use a cheaper oil," Nolan says.

"I never liked science," Glen says.

"You really do know your stuff," Kendra says.

"And sesame seed allergies are rare," the nurse says, glancing at the papers on her clipboard.

"Not as rare as marshmallow though," Nolan says. "One time at the restaurant, a kid keeled over with a marshmallow reaction."

"Oh…" Marvin says. "Can you imagine a life without s'mores?"

Glen nods. "Or hot chocolate without any marshmallows?"

Marvin points to Glen. "And rocky road ice cream?"

"All right you two, stop," Nolan says.

The nurse turns to Kendra. "You need to watch the foods you eat, all the time."

"I do!"

Glen leans in. "So you never eat a hamburger with a sesame seed bun?"

"No!"

Marvin taps Glen's shoulder. "Or Chinese food. Bet there's lots of sesame oil in that."

"You guys! I always watch everything I eat. I had no idea—"

The nurse interrupts them. "You need to rest for today and you should be fine for normal activities tomorrow." She opens the curtain and hurries away.

Kendra plants her feet on the floor and begins to stand. *What an episode.* Nolan grabs her arm to help. "Can I go up to see Ellis?" she asks him.

"Right. No…" Nolan says, balancing her as she takes a step forward. She takes a second shaky step away from the bed when someone quickly turns the corner.

"Kendra!" Matt says. His face is pale, his eyes pained. He runs to her with open arms.

Nolan lets go of her just as she reaches for Matt, falling into his arms.

"You're up? You're okay?" Matt asks.

She melts into his hold. His citrusy peppery cologne smells so calming. His arms, his love, *him!* She squeezes harder.

He buries his face in her hair and squeezes her again. "Oh baby. I'm so glad you're okay."

Marvin whispers to Glen. "Look at that."

"Clearly, she's not allergic to him," Glen whispers back.

Kendra pulls away and Matt holds her face. "I can't believe this happened. You're okay now? You feel okay?"

"I'm fine. I'm embarrassed more than anything."

"Thank God you're okay," he says again, and then wraps her in another hug.

"How'd you find us here?" Nolan asks, standing next to them.

Matt pulls away from Kendra. "Hey, you're Chef Nolan from the diner, right?" Matt extends his hand.

Nolan nods and shakes Matt's hand.

"Thank you so much for helping her," Matt says. He turns to Glen and Marvin and shakes their hands. "The paramedic that responded to the diner is a friend of mine. I just saw him out on a call and he made the connection after seeing me and Kendra at the wedding last night."

Nolan slowly crosses his arms.

Marvin clears his throat and looks to Kendra. "Well, it looks like your Prince Charming here will be your ride home, so if you don't mind, Glen and I will go up to check on Ellis."

Kendra gives Marvin a hug. "Thanks for catching me before I busted my ass." Then she turns to Glen and gives him a hug. "Thanks for doing nothing, really."

Glen gives her a squeeze. "Nobody does nothing better than

me." He looks over to Nolan. "You coming with us?"

"You bet," Nolan says. He gives Kendra a hug. "No more honey bread for you," he whispers.

Oh Nolan. Her brain says stop hugging him but her arms don't want to let him go. "Thank you for saving me and especially for staying here with me." She backs away, smiling. "Your honey bread really did taste good."

Dimples dot his cheeks. "It tasted so good, it left you speechless." Nolan looks to Matt. "You better take good care of her. I hope to see you both up at the restaurant soon." Marvin and Glen have disappeared around the curtain but Nolan gives Matt a lingering glance before he too disappears.

Matt and Kendra stand together, staring at each other. He slides his hands behind her neck, scrunching the back of her hair. "The drive here was the worst drive of my life. The thought of you being sick…scared me."

His words and his touch are making her temperature rise.

He blushes. "I know I've been busy—too busy—but that's going to change. Can I take care of you today?" he whispers.

She nods. *Yes. Today. Every day.* Her heart feels like it's smiling. "I was hoping you would."

He leans down to give her a kiss. It's slow, lingering and way more delicious than honey bread. If the hospital still had a heart monitor on her, it would have surely set off an alarm.

He wraps an arm around her shoulders and she wraps an arm around his waist. They barely take a few steps out of the room when a medical assistant rushes in, strips the sheets off of her bed and quickly begins to remake it. The nurse hurries in too, followed by a mother with four children. The children are covered in rashes: two of them have it on their faces, one on their legs and the fourth child's arms are covered with red splotches.

"I don't have an isolation ward so the best I can do is have you wait here," the nurse says as Kendra and Matt leave the room.

"Oh that looks awful," Kendra whispers to Matt.

She hadn't seen any of this medical turmoil when she arrived, but then again, she hadn't noticed much of anything. But now, she sees people sitting on the floor, leaning against walls and standing everywhere. There's a long line for the restroom and an even longer line at the receptionist counter. Sure, this is a small hospital, but this is a small town. This place should be able to handle everyone.

She grips Matt's waist with both arms as they slowly continue their walk. "What's going on here?"

He squeezes her tighter. "Just keep moving," he says. "Just keep moving."

[TWELVE]

A soft, white glow paints Kendra's bedroom with peace. Her cozy white sheets and soft, fluffy pillow envelope her body in a cushiony paradise. This long afternoon of rest has her so relaxed, she feels like she's floating. She moves her arm out from under the sheet, dangles her hand off of the bed, wiggles her fingers and waits.

Any second now…

Bingo!

A cold, wet nose rubs her fingers.

"There's my girl," she mumbles, petting Gracie's face.

Matt rolls over to see, resting his head on Kendra's shoulder. "She loves that. She loves you."

"Mmmm," Kendra moans while Gracie licks her hand. "Dog slobber on one hand and a hot man on the other: what a perfect day. Well, except for the earlier part in the hospital." She pulls her hand away from Gracie and rolls over to face the more interesting animal. Kendra and Matt lie nose-to-nose, staring at each other.

"You feeling better?" he asks, his warm, brown eyes scanning her face.

His eyes alone can make her insides melt.

"Much better," she says, biting her lower lip.

His eyebrow rises. "Oh? How much better?"

"Enough to do it again." She nips his nose and he softly groans.

The sheets crinkle as he rolls on top of her. His head lowers to hers and he gives her a slow, sensual kiss. Pleasure rolls through her.

Again. Again. Again. "Again," she whispers.

He smiles, lowers his lips for another slow kiss and soon every part of her body below her neck is quivering. She's ready. She was ready right after they did it earlier. Two kisses from this guy are all she needs to be good to go. She raises her hips. He gets the message and begins to take her.

His first push makes the room blur. She grabs his back, squeezing. Her chin rises and her eyes roll to the back of her head while pleasure begins to build inside her. Their bodies move as one, like branches in a breeze…now faster like the wind…now as feverish as a storm. She squeezes him harder and gasps in completion. He moans and slows to a stop. Their breathing is ragged, the sheets twisted into knots. A smile covers her face.

He rolls off of her, a smile covering his face too. "You feeling alright?" he whispers.

"Amazingly perfect," she whispers, cuddling to him. "Except my thigh is still a little sore and this headache hasn't gone away."

He squeezes her. "Side effects from that auto-injector thing. I'll get you some more aspirin."

She wraps her arms around him so he can't move. "Not right now. Stay here. Mmmm…in case I want to do it again."

He laughs. "Baby, I know that honey bread stuff could have

killed you but it, or something, has given you horny energy that's working for me right now."

She laughs too. "I'm just so happy to have you here…like this…next to me."

He moves strands of her hair off of her face.

"I get the feeling that days like this…having you beside me all day…will be rare," she whispers.

"I live a 24-7 job. With my situation being short-staffed and all…it's not ideal."

"I'm so confused."

"Confused? Why?"

"How can Rip be a crook that steals from the fire department when he seems so nice? I mean, I know nice people can be crooks, but Rip seems genuinely nice."

Matt sits up. She sits up too. They face each other, bare chest to bare chest.

"How do you know he's nice?" Matt asks.

"I met him, at the wedding. Him and his wife."

"Really? What'd they say?"

"They were super nice. The mayor and his wife too. Even the winery guy. He invited me back for a tour."

Matt sucks in a breath. "You met them all at the wedding? When I wasn't there?"

Sweetie, that's only part of what you missed.

"You would've been proud of me. I asked the winery guy why his vines look so dry."

Matt's face lights up. "Really? Boom! How direct! What did James say?"

"That he's concerned too and he's stumped. He's bringing some expert in to figure out what's happening."

"Please. I can see right through that. This expert will be one of James's friends, and he'll send a big bill for his services. The city will pay the bill and then his friend cashes the check and gives James a hunk of cash while nothing gets fixed at the winery."

"You really think so?"

"If I could prove it, everyone would know so."

She squirms closer. "I want to help. You're really bothered by the thought that they are criminals."

"I need proof. People like you to ask more questions. The mayor can't handle this city; Rip can't handle the fire department. I just need some way to prove it and force them out."

"I think it's already playing out, baby. I mean, hydrants are bursting every day. And look what we just saw up at the hospital. The city hospital can't even keep up with this small town!"

Matt straightens. "See? You just figured all that out, why can't everyone else? What more will it take until people demand action and force them out?" His voice is deep, his eyes hard.

She scoots even closer to him, slides her arms around his waist and presses her bare chest against his. His heart beats so fast! He'll give himself a heart attack unless he can relax!

He wraps his arms around her back, pulling her closer. His deep breathing helps to slow his racing heart.

Good.

"We'll figure it out," she whispers.

She slowly begins rocking back and forth with him. She loves every second of this: feeling her chest on his, the warmth of his skin covering her. She hates to see him so stressed; to feel his heart punishing his body. Their romance will never grow if they are surrounded by drama and if they are constantly interrupted with emergency calls. And it's not fair to the people in this city if the fire department is partially staffed! If Rip stays chief, they'll rarely have days like this together, where they can ignore the world, stay in bed and let their hands and mouths explore.

She breathes in, filling her lungs with purpose. She can dig deeper. She can ask questions. Why not? After all, she took a bold start by confronting the group at the wedding. Now it's time to go further. For Matt's sake.

A shiver slices through her body; her subconscious sending her a message. More like a warning. She's done this before. She dug deeper to try to find answers to help her lover. Her lover was Christopher. She stuck her nose where it wasn't supposed to be and found out things she wasn't supposed to know. *Have you not learned?*

Gently, she and Matt continue to rock back and forth, content to be in each other's arms.

This is different. Matt wants help. Matt needs help! Christopher didn't want anything from her. But she set off on a mission to try to help him anyway. And in the process, she lost him. And one day if the video ever comes out, she could lose it all.

The video. Christopher. The wedding.

She takes a hard swallow. "Something else happened at the wedding that I wanted to tell you about," she whispers.

He stops rocking. "What?"

"My ex showed up."

He drops his arms. "Your ex? Like unannounced and uninvited?"

"His sister is friends with Susan, so unfortunately she came. And he drove her."

"What did he want?" Matt sits up straight.

"To remind me what a good decision it was to leave him."

Matt looks to the ceiling. "Thank goodness he didn't come to try to win you back. Especially when I wasn't there! Where does he live anyway?"

"Richmond. Far enough that I shouldn't see him again."

Matt looks to his lap. She looks down too, and then gently pokes him in the chest.

"So, who was your last girlfriend?"

His eyes roll. "A drama queen named Brenda. God, she doesn't even compare to you. Best day of my life is when she left."

"Well if you wanted her gone, why wait for her to leave?"

"It was complicated."

Kendra looks back down. Yeah, she understands complicated.

Silence fills her bedroom.

Should she bring up the video now? Or is this too early in the relationship?

She looks up and then kisses his cheek, gently and loving. She's just getting to know him. They've never spent as much time together as they have today. Leave it alone. Don't scare him away. Or even worse: make him mad enough to find Christopher and confront him.

Matt's smile grows with each of her kisses. This—them—is the topic to stay on today. From the moment she first saw Matt, she's wanted his boots at the door and his jeans on her floor. And now, she's got him. Heaven is in her arms. And if getting more time with him means she must expose a crime to get it, then that's what she'll do.

He rolls his head and gently kisses her ear.

She turns, making them face-to-face. Her mouth stretches in a wide smile. "Again?" she whispers.

His chin lowers and his eyes seem to twinkle. "It's gotta be the fucking honey bread."

And then he gives her what she wants.

[THIRTEEN]

C lick, off.

Click, on.

Click, off.

Kendra sighs, her elbows planted on her desk, her head resting in one fisted hand while she holds a cheap Oak Bank ink pen in the other. She stares out the bank window at the breezy, sunny day.

Click, on.

Click, off. Off. *Off?*

She glares at the pen. That's the second one that's broken this morning. She tosses it in the trash and picks up another one.

Click, on.

A customer walks away from the teller counter and heads for the door, passing Kendra's desk.

Kendra sits up straight. "Have a nice day," she says, smiling. She watches the lady leave and then looks around the branch.

No customers.

Click, off.

Outside, a stiff wind blows a pile of leaves and Kendra's eyes wander back out the window again. Leaves in beautiful shades of oranges, reds and browns tumble through the empty front spaces of the parking lot. They surrender themselves to the wind like they don't have a care in the world.

Lucky leaves.

Click, on.

If she were a leaf, she'd probably blow right into Christopher's trendy neighborhood off of Grove Street in Richmond. She'd land on the manicured lawn, where, with her luck, Portia would spot her and demand that the lawn crew mow her over. That is, if Portia didn't first grind her into the ground with her Prada heels.

Click, off.

After Saturday's run-in with Portia and Christopher, Kendra needs a plan. Her wishful thinking that Christopher would do the right thing and erase the tape after she left apparently didn't happen. Now that she knows he has no intention of getting rid of it, there must be some other way to get that video back, along with any copies he may have made. Her promise to never tell his secret isn't good enough. She's got to raise the stakes. Maybe get something else on him. Or Portia.

Click, on.

Outside, another gust of wind lifts a big pile of leaves, catching Kendra's eye. The leaves swirl angrily in the air and then smack right into the side of Kendra's Audi.

Click, off.

Perfect. What a perfect illustration of how stupid it would be to dig up more dirt on Christopher. She'd probably get caught by Portia or one of her well-to-do, super-connected friends and end up smacked like those leaves just got whacked on the side of her car. What he's doing is illegal. She doesn't need more dirt. She should turn him in. What are the chances that he hits "send" on her embarrassing video before he's dragged to jail?

Click, on.

Does Portia even know about the video? Sure, Portia's in on his crime—hell—she *helped* him with it, but does she know what Christopher has on her? Would a brother tell his sister *that*?

Kendra hears a giggle behind the teller counter and looks to see Marley intently looking down at something. She's probably watching a funny video on her phone. Kendra's stomach tightens, just like yesterday morning when she sat alone at Seven Spoons wondering if—and when—the guys in the diner might ever see her video. How can she live her life like this?

Mrs. Danner is still behind the closed door of her office, the blinds on the glass wall pulled shut. And that's not really a bad thing. Kendra had hoped for a slow Monday to help her recover from yesterday's embarrassing sesame seed collapse, plus her energetic yet restful afternoon in bed with Matt, but this branch is way too slow.

Cindy walks toward Kendra, holding a folder. She wears a burgundy suit with a slender pencil skirt and pearls at her neck. She pulls out a chair in front of Kendra's desk.

"Feel okay to do this now?" Cindy asks, taking a seat.

Kendra clicks off the pen. "We don't have time to wait," she says, looking around the empty branch. "And I feel fine after my episode yesterday, so yes, let's meet now."

"I like that you moved your desk out here," Cindy says.

"Me too. It's hard to meet people and cross-sell products from that back office. And when someone comes to do a loan, I can go back there for privacy if I need to. That is, if anyone ever comes in for a loan." She shuffles some papers and pulls out a blank one. "Okay, let's brainstorm ideas to get more traffic in here."

Cindy's eyes flick down and then back up. "First, if you don't mind, I was wondering: are you okay after that argument you had with that guy at the wedding on Saturday?"

Kendra clicks the pen on and off, twice.

"Sorry you had to see that. By the way, your timing when asking me to leave was perfect."

"I didn't know I was rescuing you at the time but I'm glad I could help. You never did tell me who he was."

Kendra exhales. "An ex. A doctor. In Richmond. One that shouldn't be back in this town, like ever."

"Everything okay between the two of you?"

"No, and it probably won't be. But thanks for asking."

"I still can't believe you came in this morning after being in the hospital yesterday."

"Really, I was only there a few hours. I was fine. Well, once Chef Nolan saved my life and stuff."

"Chef is the nicest guy. A good cook too! He made me a double-crust apple pie on my birthday."

"He really is nice. He sat with me and held my hand, until Matt came to drive me home."

Cindy's face stretches with a smirk. She's always so prim and proper at work—what's with this look?

"What? You look like you thought of something funny."

She nods, with a school-girl, playful grin. "Do you realize, since Saturday night you've been closely involved with a doctor, a chef and a fireman?"

Kendra shrugs. "Yeah, I guess. And?"

"And a doctor, a chef and a fireman happened to be the first three months of my *Red Hot American Men* wall calendar."

Kendra bursts into a laugh. "You have a hot men wall calendar?"

Cindy shimmies. "Yeah, in the back room, by my desk. You haven't noticed? This month is a postman."

Marley hollers out from behind the teller counter, "My favorite was June and the policeman." She fans herself.

Cindy nods. "Yes indeed. He was good."

Kendra rests her hand on her forehead. First, she saw Cindy half drunk on Saturday night, and now this? Oh the joy of getting to know co workers. She looks back up.

"Okay, you guys. Unless we're going to do a bank calendar with local hot men as a promotional gimmick, we need to shift this conversation and brainstorm on how to get more men and women—hot or not—into this branch."

"Well, you can never go wrong with free food," Cindy says.

"Absolutely. Especially cake. Cake and coffee or punch is cheap and easy. What can we celebrate with a cake?"

"Fall?" Marley calls out.

"The upcoming holidays?" Kendra asks.

"A kick-off to the holiday season?" Cindy asks.

Kendra sits back and clicks her pen again. "I like that! And the end of October is a perfect time. A savings checkup and get your loan for big gift items, like a car."

"Or jewelry!"

Marley shouts from behind the counter. "Or appliances!"

"Heck, I'm ready to write a loan for anything," Kendra says. She wrinkles her eyebrows and turns to Marley. "Appliances?

Maybe a home equity loan, but appliances?"

"Well, I need a loan for a new washing machine," Marley says with a heavy sigh. "I live in my mom's old house, up by Travis Pond, and her old machine went out on me this weekend. Now I'll have to go to the laundromat way over on Maple Street until I can afford to buy a new one."

Kendra gives an understanding nod. Not good for Marley. It's hard to get by on a teller's salary. The few bonuses tellers can earn have never happened at this branch. Kendra will be lucky to get her own bonus unless things pick up. But at least she's managed her money well, socking it away for emergencies and even putting extra money away for fashion splurges. Right now, she's almost got enough money saved to buy a pair of *So Kate* Christian Louboutin black pumps.

She swivels on her chair to face Cindy again. "Okay, so Marley needs to hit her teller goal, quick, and I sure want to hit my own sales goal and I'm guessing you do too, so let's launch a plan to get some life and business back into this place."

"Agreed!" Cindy says.

The sound of the outside wind comes rushing in with the opening door. James, the winery owner, walks in.

Kendra clicks her ink pen off and on a couple of times. Just what she needs: a morning with one of the town's alleged crooks. She plasters on a smile and stands. "Good morning! Surviving the wind out there?"

James approaches her desk, just as Cindy stands to greet him too. "You should feel the wind up at the winery," he says. "The few leaves we had on the vines are struggling to stay on!"

Kendra's eyes narrow. *Spend some money on watering, champ, and those leaves might have a chance.*

"What can I help you with today?" she asks.

He points to her desk. "Hey, I like your desk out here. It's nice to see your smiling face when I walk in!"

Kendra gestures with both hands to the desk below. "Out here is the best way for me to meet our customers."

James nods. "Very smart! Well, I came in today because I need to get a new loan."

Kendra straightens. *A loan? Him?* Her interest is piqued as high as when the September issue of *Vogue* arrives. "I can help you with that. A loan for the winery? Or personal?"

"Well hello!" a voice calls from behind them. Mrs. Danner has opened her door is stepping into the lobby. "Dear James, what a pleasure!"

He steps toward her with a wide smile. "Louise!" They embrace. "How is your Monday morning going?"

She dips her chin to her chest. "Lovely now that you're here. How can I help you?"

"I was speaking to Kendra here about a loan."

"Of course!" she says, sweeping him toward her office with one arm. "Come to my office and I'll help you."

The two walk away, into Mrs. Danner's office, and the door closes. Cindy and Kendra stand abandoned in the lobby.

"What was that?" Cindy asks. "You do the loans now, we all know that. What's she doing?"

Kendra grinds her teeth and stares at Louise Danner's closed office door. She swept him away so fast, it's like she's helping him keep a secret. Why else wouldn't she let her help him? *Whatever.* It won't be a secret for long. By tomorrow, or even tonight, Kendra will be able to see in the system what type of loan he's getting. If it's a personal loan, that's one thing. If he's taking out a loan for the winery, that might be suspicious, especially if they really have plenty of money from the city's tourism tax. Either way, how's she supposed to meet her sales goals if the boss swipes loans right out from under her?

Kendra turns to face Cindy. "Let's get back to discussing cake."

Cindy shakes her head. Just as they sit down, the branch door opens again. A delivery man wrestles a huge bouquet of red roses inside, struggling against the wind.

Cindy leans over Kendra's desk. "I don't think those are for me."

The delivery man looks at Kendra. "You're Kendra King, right?"

"Uh-huh."

He places the vase on her desk. "For you. Have a nice day!" He turns and leaves.

"Wow, they're beautiful," Kendra says, sniffing the roses. She takes out the card.

Honey bread for days. Sesame-seed free, of course.
Happy Monday.
Matt

Oh my word. Her smile spreads. She folds the card and tucks it into her drawer. No way does she want *that* card on display for everyone else to see.

"Are the flowers from the fireman?" Cindy asks. "They shouldn't be from the doctor. And they wouldn't be from the chef…"

Kendra laughs. "And since I don't know this month's hot

American postman, it couldn't be him. I've never met the policeman from June either. So yeah, good guess: they're from the fireman alright."

Cindy and Kendra begin to sit back down but the branch door swings open again. In walks a tall, older gentleman, wearing a jacket with a pink polo shirt.

"Glen?" Kendra asks, straightening.

"Hey," Glen says, twisting his hands and walking toward her.

"I'll be right back," Cindy says and steps away.

Glen's usual sarcastic smile has been wiped from his face. He looks to the left and then the right.

"You okay?" Kendra asks.

"Me? Fine. Hey, how are you?"

"I'm fine. I rested a lot yesterday. Well, sort of. So what brings you in here?"

"We thought we'd see you at breakfast today."

Heh. Her breakfast this morning was another serving of Matt. "I stayed in bed a little longer this morning."

His eyes graze the floor.

"You sure you're okay, Glen?"

He glances up. "Me? Yeah. Fine. It's just, we thought you would want to know. Ellis didn't do so good last night. He's taken a turn for the worse."

Her jaw slackens. "Oh no."

"They released him yesterday and we got him home and he seemed to get worse. We took him back up to the hospital late last night. I'm on my way up there now. Nolan's coming when he gets off at the diner."

"Is his body just failing? What's wrong?"

"That's the thing. None of us can get any answers. It's his heart, that's all we know."

There's no joking today. Jovial Glen has checked his humor at the hospital door. This must be serious, for him to act like this and for him to come here to tell her.

"I know you asked about him a couple of times yesterday," Glen says. "So I thought you would want to know."

Kendra nods. "Yeah, I want to know. He has no family! I mean, I don't know him well, but no one deserves to be alone when they're sick. I'll come up after work." She turns to the teller counter. "Marley? Did you hear this?"

"This is awful!" Marley says. "I want to see him too, but I can't come up tonight. Maybe I'll go before work tomorrow."

Kendra nods and turns back to Glen. "Is there anything I can bring tonight?"

Glen shakes his head. "He stopped eating last night. Nolan couldn't even get him to eat his chicken soup."

She reaches for Glen's shoulder and squeezes him. "Thanks for telling me. I'll get up there as soon as I can."

Glen nods. "Nolan thought you might."

Kendra smiles. Her friends from the diner have pretty much figured her out.

Glen turns to leave.

"Wait!" Kendra pulls a rose from her vase and hands it to him. "Give this to Ellis and tell him a mysterious woman will be visiting him tonight. Maybe he'll get a kick out of that."

"He's gonna love it!" Marley says.

Glen takes the rose. "You kidding? This will perk him up."

"Good! Tell him he has to eat dinner before the mysterious woman visits."

"That's an even better ruse. I like the clever way you think."

Kendra nods. "Thanks for coming to tell me, Glen."

He begins to walk away. "See you tonight."

He pushes open the door to leave and another cold wind blows in. Kendra glances outside, watching Glen get into his car.

Why is old man Ellis so suddenly, and seriously, sick?

"Hey Kendra," Cindy calls out from across the lobby, "look at this."

Cindy stands under a television set mounted on the wall, pointing to the local noon news program. Kendra walks over and squints to see.

It's a story about an elementary school, doing a fall festival. "Look," Cindy says, "a cake walk! Everyone loves cake, right?"

The live shot shows children walking around a circle to the lively beat of music. They step on numbers painted on the floor when suddenly the music stops and they all look down.

"Number thirty-two!" an emcee announces.

A little girl standing on number thirty-two screams and then runs to a table full of cakes, choosing her prize. She turns to face the camera with a wide, rosy smile, holding up a round, strawberry-frosted cake loaded with colorful sprinkles.

Cindy points to the TV. "I bet that cake gets eaten by the time she gets on the bus to go home."

Kendra nods to Cindy. "So, do you want to do a cake walk, in the branch?"

Cindy laughs. "I don't know but maybe we could try…"

Kendra looks back up at the television and immediately tunes Cindy out. The reporter has pulled one of the festival attendees for a live interview. It's Mayor Tony Fletcher!

Kendra takes a step closer to the television to hear.

"Mayor Fletcher, it's good to see you out here for the children, but can you comment on why Cory City's fire hydrants keep bursting?" a female TV reporter asks.

Tony looks right at the camera, eyes wide. "We've got years of upgrading to do and that takes time and money."

The reporter presses on, unflustered, even while children run around them. "Why hasn't the city kept up with maintenance?"

He flashes a politician's smile. "I'm here today to support the children and this wonderful festival they've worked so hard on."

"But mayor, there have been reports that the winery will be asking the city for additional funding next year. Won't that keep money from other important city projects?"

"Well, the winery is important…"

"And several residents have complained that…"

Kendra sweeps her arm in the air. "Grab my phone. Please! Fast!" Cindy dashes over to Kendra's desk.

"…wait times at the hospital are long and sick people are not being treated quickly enough," the reporter continues.

The mayor looks straight into the camera. "Running a city takes a lot of resources…"

"Here!" Cindy says, handing Kendra her phone.

Kendra quickly types a text to Matt.

Quick! Ch 12 news! Now!

She hits send, her hands shaking. Hopefully he's at the fire station, near a TV. This is what he's been waiting for! Finally, someone is asking questions!

"…let's all support the Cory City Elementary fall festival today!" the mayor says, curtly nodding to the reporter that he's finished with this interview. He walks away and the camera shifts to the reporter.

"That's Cory City Mayor Tony Fletcher, explaining, somewhat, why this small town is facing so many challenges. For Richmond's KWBG, I'm Stephanie Parker. Mike, back to you."

The camera cuts to a man at the news desk, where he continues the news.

"Wow," Kendra mutters. Her phone buzzes with a text from Matt.

Something wrong?

No, something right! Mayor just got grilled on live TV! Richmond station covering CC elementary carnival.

Seriously! Was it good?

She asked ?s he didn't answer. Try to find a way to watch it.

I will! Tks!

Kendra smiles and texts him one more time.

Honey bread AND roses for days. Thank you.

It may be her imagination but her phone feels hotter in her hands while she watches the screen and the pulsing three dots as he types his reply.

You are the best thing that has happened to me. Roses every week is the least I can do.

She holds her phone to her chest and then types a single emoji reply.

[FOURTEEN]

Kendra's only taken a few steps away from her car but already her nose, throat and lungs feel frozen. If she could have skipped the end-of-the-day lecture from Mrs. Danner, she would have reached Cory City Hospital sooner. She was lucky to find a parking space, even if it's in the grassy back lot. She hurries to the main entrance as fast as her Vince Camuto suede boots will let her go.

The double doors swoosh open and Kendra runs into a madhouse.

No receptionist staffs the desk, even though it's only 6:30 p.m. Every chair in the waiting room is taken and several people are sitting on end tables or on the floor.

A nurse comes out of the emergency room and calls out a name from a list. A young family steps forward, a baby wrapped in blankets in the mother's arms.

Kendra quickly finds the elevator and presses the call button. She found out yesterday that this two-story hospital is a regional facility that Richmond General operates and is partially funded by Cory City. With only twenty-four beds, it's supposed to be big enough for this city. But apparently not today. Or yesterday.

The elevator arrives. Kendra steps inside and a few others follow.

Once they reach the second floor, Kendra looks for a directional sign to steer her to room seventeen, where Ellis is supposed to be. Two people are standing in the hall, blocking her view of the sign. This isn't that big of a place, so she sets off to find the room herself.

She heads down a hallway, busy with people walking around. An empty gurney waits against a wall and a medical cart is pushed against the opposite wall. This hall is beginning to feel like a storage unit. She passes an open door to a room when suddenly a woman screams.

"Help! Doctor! Help!"

Kendra stops cold and looks inside. A little boy is violently convulsing on a bed. The woman tries to hold him down while she screams. "Help!"

A doctor rushes past Kendra, his white coat a blur as he runs into the room. "Get me Ativan!" he yells. A nurse follows with a medical bag.

Kendra can't move. She feels like she's stuck inside a glass train that's derailed and heading for a cliff. *That boy! His poor mother!*

The doctor rolls the boy on to his side. "Hold on, Joey. Hold on…" the doctor says, and the boy's convulsions begin to slow until finally his feet stop thrashing.

"Oh thank God! Thank you!" the mother calls out. "Joey—baby—mommy's here."

Kendra grabs her face, chills spiraling down her spine. She closes her eyes. *Thank you, Lord, for keeping that boy safe. Please comfort his mother. God bless the staff trying to help this mess.*

She opens her eyes, blurry with shock, just as the doctor comes out of the room.

What if that boy had died? Right here? And she saw it? *Please God help him get better.* Kendra can't even see straight. Still clutching her face, she's vaguely aware that the doctor is walking closer. Then her eyes snap into focus in time for her to see…

Blond hair, thick and stylishly swept to the side.

Blue eyes.

Christopher?

Her eyes cross.

"Kendra?" Christopher asks, reaching for her shoulder.

She shakes off her shock. "What the hell are you doing here?"

"What are *you* doing here? Are you sick too?" Christopher asks, his eyes worried.

She shakes her head. "I live here. This is my town. You don't live here. Why are you here?"

Christopher steers her near a wall. He looks to either side and then leans closer. "I was called in to help. This is an affiliate hospital of ours, remember?"

She shakes her head in little, jerky movements. "No. No. You can't be here."

"It's okay. I know what I'm doing."

"No. No. People are sick here. Really sick. You shouldn't be here. You work in a lab. You told me you only worked in a hospital lab!"

Christopher leans closer, squinting. "Kendra, there's a problem and I'm here to help. I can help."

She can't stop shaking her head. "No, no. This has gone too far." Her body feels like it's on fire, hot with anger.

"Calm down, Kendra. I know what I'm doing," he whispers.

No! "How can you know what you're doing? You're not even a damn doctor!"

He yanks her arm and pulls her closer. "Now is not the fucking time."

"Stop now, Christopher. Give it up. Run away and never come back. Don't try to pretend you can help these people."

His eyes ignite. "I am helping these people. I know more about medicine than the clowns that work here. This place is a fucking mess, Kendra. A fucking, small town mess."

"This is ridiculous."

He squeezes her arm. "No, it's not. I was only one semester short in medical school. I knew what I needed to know. I'm not proud of what I did but I'm here. And right now, I know more than these idiots."

"No, you're the idiot, pretending to be a doctor. And I'm an idiot for keeping your stupid secret."

"Well, keep it longer because right now, I have lives to save."

He drops her arm and gives her a searing stare.

"Doctor?" a voice calls out from down the hall.

Christopher's head turns. "Be right there."

Kendra feels plastered to the wall, flattened by his stare, reduced by the truth. This cannot be happening! Christopher walks away from her, quickly moving to the end of the hall where an older woman stands in the doorway. Her face lights up with relief. "Thank you, Doctor. If you could just check…" And the two disappear into a room.

He said he worked in a lab! She knew he hadn't finished medical school. She knew Portia had one of her sketchy friends forge his graduation records and residency. But she didn't know he was practicing with real people! She kept his secret because she didn't think people would get hurt. Plus he was blackmailing her! Now he's running around, flaunting the fraud that he is and she's just as guilty!

"Kendra?" a man's voice asks.

She looks up to see Marvin, his face pale, his expression grim, just like his brother Glen earlier today. "Marv?" She wills her softened legs to stand stronger and pulls her shoulders back. *Focus. Just keep pretending.*

"Have you gone down there yet?" Marvin points down the hall.

"No, I was heading there," she says, beginning to walk down the hall with him. They pass the room Christopher disappeared into and she leans to look in. Christopher is standing next to an older man, who is lying in his bed. Christopher's smiling a confident, cocktail-party, politician's smile and gripping the patient's hand. *Oh God.*

Marvin steers her to the room across the hall. Nolan leans against a wall inside the room, his eyes worried, his face unshaven. He straightens when he sees Kendra and runs his hand through his jet-black hair.

"Hey," she whispers. They share a quick hug. "How's everyone doing?" She takes another step inside, closer to Ellis's bed.

Ellis cracks his eyes open. His skin is ashen, his face and hands bloated. But he's still wearing his World War II baseball cap.

"I knew it was gonna be you," he mumbles. "The beautiful woman who gave me the flower."

She looks at his bedside table, where the rose sits in a plastic cup of water.

Precious. She gently picks up his hand. *So cold.* "How many beautiful women have given you a flower before?"

"Awww…too many to tell you."

Marvin and Nolan chuckle.

"The women never give me flowers," Glen says from the chair next to the bed. "How come you get so many?"

Ellis blinks a few times. "I look better," he slowly says, and then he closes his eyes.

Kendra leans closer to look him over. "He's asleep? Just like that?"

Nolan nods. "Just like that. He wakes up, cracks a few funny lines and falls back asleep."

Kendra strokes his hand. His fingers are so swollen, his entire hand so puffy. Oh the life of stories this man must have. But how sad is it that she knows none of them. *Time.* It really doesn't take much time to visit with people, talk to people and learn about their lives. Or even to be there when they die. Just a few years ago it was time that kept her from her own grandpa the night he died. She was right across town too, studying for a final exam at Richmond University. She didn't have time to go up to the hospital on the night he was brought in, when he was having trouble breathing. "It's fine," her mother told her. "Come up when you can." But that night, he died. She didn't get to hold his hand, stroke his skin or give him a rose. She squeezes Ellis's hand again and turns to Nolan. "So, he has no kids? Nieces or nephews?"

Nolan nods. "We tracked down a nephew in West Virginia. He's called me a couple of times today. He's the only close relative."

"I don't get why he's on such a roller coaster," Kendra says.

"He improves when he's here. He gets sicker when he's home," Nolan says, head tilted, looking him over.

"It's gotta be something at home making him sick. Mold or allergies making his heart weak?"

Suddenly, the heartbeat monitor sounds an alarm. All colored lines—green, red, beige, blue, white, purple—go flat. Ellis's face goes slack. Kendra drops his hand and flies backward. Nolan rushes to Ellis's side as Marvin runs out the door, yelling for help.

A nurse runs in, grabbing the paddles of the cardiac defibrillator. "Come on!" she yells, struggling with the machine.

The alarm screeches as the nurse wrestles with the defibrillator.

Kendra runs out of the room. *God help her...she needs Christopher. Now!* She thrusts herself into the doorway of every room until finally, she sees him running towards her. "I need you!" she yells.

He runs past her, heading straight to the sound of the alarm. She's at his heels as he rounds the corner, sprinting into Ellis's room.

"Defib?" he yells.

"It's not powering on!" the nurse yells.

Christopher jumps on the bed, straddling Ellis's body and begins CPR. "Five...six...seven," he says, counting every compression.

The nurse pushes down on Ellis's forehead with one hand and uses her other to raise his throat. She counts with Christopher. "Twenty-nine...thirty."

"Go!" Christopher yells and the nurse pinches Ellis's nose and gives two quick blows into his mouth.

Christopher rises up to begin compressions again when Ellis suddenly coughs. The alarm stops screeching and the machine begins a series of steady beeps. The colored lines resume a jagged, pulsing pattern. Ellis coughs again.

"Open his airway again," Christopher says and the nurse again tilts Ellis's head back so his airway is clear. Christopher jumps off of the bed and begins examining Ellis's pupils. He works around Ellis's body, checking his pulse, reading the monitor.

Another nurse rushes into the room, also assisting. After several minutes, Christopher turns to Nolan, Kendra, Marvin and Glen, who stand flat against the wall in shocked silence. "He's stable. But we need to move him to the bigger hospital in Richmond."

All four nod.

The nurse continues checking Ellis over and Christopher walks to the foot of the bed. Marvin and Glen move past him, to Ellis's head, leaving Christopher, Nolan and Kendra by the end of the bed.

"Is he going to be okay?" Kendra whispers, her heart thumping hard with adrenaline. "Why can't anyone figure out what's wrong with him?"

Christopher's cheeks pulse. "I looked at his records earlier. Obviously, what you just saw was heart failure, but what led to it is what's making most all of these people sick."

Nolan leans closer. "Most all of these people?"

Christopher's eyes shift left and right. He nods to the corner, by the door. Nolan and Kendra follow him.

"When I got here this morning, I immediately noticed a trend," Christopher says. "It's the young and the old that are sick, with varying symptoms. Heart failure, rashes, seizures, one kid even slipped into a coma…"

Kendra clutches her stomach.

"They weren't running blood tests on everyone here. Simple blood tests. I don't know if it's because they're overwhelmed or if it's because they're just stupid. So I ordered them on every patient and had my friends back in the lab run a comparison."

"You think there's one thing in common?" Nolan asks.

"I know there's one thing," Christopher says.

Suddenly the door opens, nearly crushing Nolan, Kendra and Christopher behind it. "We need you, stat!" a nurse calls out.

Christopher nods, already stepping to the door. Kendra grabs his arm. "Wait! Tell us!"

He leans closer to her and Nolan. "I don't know why or how, but most everyone in here is suffering from an overexposure to sodium chloride."

Nolan straightens. "Wait. That would explain why—"

"I have to go," Christopher says, already out the door.

Kendra stares at the floor. *Matt.* "Matt's been saying something's going on."

"Matt? Does he know something?" Nolan asks.

Her eyes snap up. *No!* She can't let Christopher leave yet. Kendra bolts out of the room and sees him down the hall. In a few quick steps she has him within reach and tugs his elbow. He turns.

Her eyes brim with tears. "You saved him. You were right. You do know what you're doing."

His eyes tear up too.

"I'm sorry," she whispers. "I'm sorry I didn't think you knew anything."

"I made a mistake, Kendee. I didn't graduate. I know this isn't right. But if you were in my shoes…with the pressure from my father…one lie led to another. One day, I'll make it right. But now…"

"Doctor!" a woman yells from down the hall.

Kendra grabs his hands. "Thank you."

He squeezes her and then drops her hands. He begins to move away but he stops and turns back to face her.

The weight of his stare reminds her of every reason why she fell for him. If she wasn't so angry…so disgusted by his lying and blackmailing…she'd be tempted to grab his head and cover his face with hungry kisses. The way she did before. The way they both did, back then.

"You should know," he says, loud enough for only her to hear. "I deleted it. The day you left, I got rid of it."

The video?

He turns and hurries away, leaving Kendra clutching her chest, standing in the middle of the hall.

He got rid of it?

Breath is hard for her to find. The ups and downs of this night have her heart and brain reeling. People pass her in the hall, their expression stressed and exhausted. She's stuck in place, like a pinball wedged in a corner, while the paddles of life swat around her. It doesn't seem real that any of tonight can be happening.

It's gone? The video is really gone? She's free?

She looks to the floor. *And he said…what? Sodium chloride? Ellis and these people are sick because they ate too much…salt?*

Someone taps her shoulder. "Hey," Nolan says. "You okay?"

She turns around. He's got his leather jacket on and a scarf around his neck.

"I…I…don't know," she mutters. "You're…leaving?"

He pulls the ends of his scarf, tightening it around his neck. His face is taught, his cheeks pulse and his eyes burn. *Nolan? Angry?*

"I'm leaving. And you should come with me."

[FIFTEEN]

The full moon fills the night sky with an eerie orange glow. Scruffy roadside brush speeds by in a blur as Nolan sails down Route 5. Kendra squeezes the armrest of his Ford truck and leans into a turn.

Nolan flicks her a glance. "Sorry about that." He grips the wheel with both hands as he comes out of the turn.

"I've never been on this part of Route 5," she says.

"It's the fastest way to get to Ellis's house."

She swallows hard. "You still haven't told me what we're looking for."

He nods, the silhouette of his face outlined against the moon's light. She hasn't seen his dimples all night. "I'm not sure I could even get the words out of my mouth if I tried," he says. "After what your doctor friend said, I just want to go back and look at something."

The road narrows, surrounded by fields of tall corn, gently bending with the cold, evening breeze. Kendra peers through the windshield at the moon. "It's like it's as bright as day outside, only orange."

Nolan nods. "It's a late harvest moon this year. Happens

every couple of years in October. Around here, we call it a wine moon."

Kendra smiles. "Because this is when the grapes are supposed to be harvested? If the winery had grapes?"

"Something like that."

Kendra pulls her phone from her purse and checks her messages. No evening message from Matt and she's not sure how or if she should tell him what she's up to. "You know, Matt's been saying something is going on in this town too," she says, putting her phone back in her purse. "He's not a fan of his boss Rip, or the mayor, or even James, the winery owner."

"You mentioned that up at the hospital, which is one reason why I wanted you to come with me. What exactly does Matt think?"

"He thinks they're pocketing taxpayer money. But what would that have to do with people getting sick? Is the city water station not being maintained or something?"

Nolan takes another sharp turn. "Think about it. The hospital is fine. Seven Spoons is fine. My apartment is fine, probably yours too. It's not the city water."

Gravel grinds under his tires as he turns into a driveway lined with a wooden post fence. Ellis's small beige house stands far away from the road, all alone. Nolan's headlights shine ahead on the gravel drive and the house slowly comes into better view. Wildflowers grow against the white wood siding and the overhang sags above a faded-red door. The gravel driveway ends at a dented garage door and Kendra already has her hand on the door handle, ready to get out as soon as Nolan parks.

"Hold on," he says, speeding up and heading straight for a bed of small landscape rocks.

"What the…"

His tires gobble up the rocks, the cab bounces and in seconds they've gone up and over the rocky bed, emerging in a grassy field and driving toward a patch of trees.

"Okay, so that wasn't as easy as I thought," he says, gripping the wheel.

"You picked an odd night for a joy-ride." She squeezes the handle now.

His lights sweep over the stubbly grass, shining on a cluster of bare oak and maple trees. The truck comes to a stop and he puts the truck in park. "Ready for an adventure?"

Her head slowly turns to him. *Yes. No.* "Why are we here?"

"Come on," he says, opening his door.

She's still in the skirt and blouse she's been wearing all day and her sweater has no pockets. No way is she leaving this truck without her phone, especially to go off into the woods with a man she trusts, but really, doesn't know well. She squeezes her phone and slowly opens her door. Nolan has already walked around the truck to help her out. "Will you be okay walking in your boots out here?" he asks.

She looks down at her suede boots. "As long as we're not in the mud, sure." He extends a hand and she takes it. "Are we looking for something?"

He leads her to the front of the truck, where the lights still shine on the trees ahead. "Look at this." He points to a space beyond the trees. A few steps later, she sees it.

"Tire tracks?"

"Yeah," he says, still leading her by the hand. "And look." He drops her hand and points beyond the trees. "Those tracks lead straight to the pond."

"Who would have driven a truck up here?" she asks. "Someone fishing?"

"I don't think so. You have to drive up and over those rocks, like we just did, and that's hard to do towing a trailer. To get a truck down here, you have to really want to trespass. And I don't think many people even know about this pond."

"Look," she says, taking a few steps and looking around. "There's another set."

Nolan nods. "That's what I wanted to see. I saw the first set on Saturday, when I visited Ellis before the wedding. Then I thought I saw another set when we were here yesterday. I didn't think much of it, until now." He walks closer to the edge of the pond. "See? They go right down to the water's edge, like someone's launching a boat."

"But they couldn't get a boat back here, with those rocks."

"Exactly. Come on. Let's go up to the house." Nolan opens her door and they both get back into the truck. "Buckle up," he says as soon as he gets behind the wheel.

He makes a sharp turn and heads for the landscape rocks. Kendra grips the door armrest. Several jarring bounces later, they're back on the gravel driveway, out of the truck and heading for the front door. Nolan bends down and lifts up a clay flower pot filled with dirt. Under it is a key. He unlocks the door, they step inside and he flips on an overhead light.

A small blue plaid couch with a knitted throw blanket is centered in the small room, facing a stone fireplace. Black and white photographs in wooden frames line the mantel and Kendra can't resist taking a look. She steps closer. "She's beautiful. Was this his wife?"

Nolan's at her shoulder. "Yeah, Millie. She died…maybe ten

years ago. I never knew her, but I sure have seen this photo. He carries a copy in his wallet and he'll show you every time you ask to see it."

Kendra smiles. That's exactly what she'll do next time she sees him.

"Come on, I want to go to the garage," he says, walking out of the room. She follows him and as he walks away, her eyes can't help it: she gives a once-over glance at Nolan's jeans. He's wearing the same pair he wore the day they first met, when she nicknamed him "chef-awesome-jeans". She quickly looks away. *Geez, girl.* She's got a boyfriend, she's in a crisis, she's in a stranger's house and yet her eyes are glued to Nolan's ass. *Stop.*

She follows him into the kitchen, where a clean plate and fork sit beside the sink, next to an empty take-out food container. Whatever was in that container—or might still be in there—smells pungent. Small windows with white, eyelet café curtains surround a table with two chairs, set with one empty placemat.

"He keeps a clean kitchen," she says, "except for not taking out the trash."

Nolan tosses the take-out container into a garbage can next to the sink. "He eats a lot of take-out food, but it's from my place or other decent restaurants in town. And he eats really healthy. I don't think food gives him enough sodium to make him sick."

Kendra points to the garbage can. "We should take that with us since he's probably not going to be back for a while."

Nolan opens the door leading to the garage, turns on the light, and they step into a tool-collector's paradise. "Whoa," she says. Wooden workbenches line the garage walls, each with a theme: power tools, hand tools and more. Loose tools hang from neatly organized pegboard hooks. The power saws sit plugged in, ready to go. There's even one bench stacked with drawers filled with washers, nuts and screws. "It's like a tool museum. He probably hasn't used these in years," she says.

"Looking at these is what makes him happy," he says.

Parked perfectly in the middle of the garage is his silver four-door sedan. Kendra grins. "Look. He can center his car in this small garage but he can't get half of his car into the wide-open disabled space at Seven Spoons."

"I know, right?" Nolan says. He points to a pressure tank in the corner. "There. Right there. That's what I wanted to see."

"He has a well?"

"I didn't know for sure but it looks like he's not on city water." He faces her with busy, searching eyes. She's seen this look before, at the diner, when he's juggling orders and thinking fast on his feet. Doing several things at once is easy for him and right now, his brain appears to be on overload.

"Oh my God," he whispers, staring her straight in the eye.

"Someone tampered with his well?"

"I think someone tampered with his pond!"

Kendra straightens.

"If high sodium is aggravating his heart condition, and knowing how healthy he eats, he's got to be getting high doses of sodium from more than food. It's got to be what he's drinking too."

"That pond has too much salt?"

"This pond backs up to the Whitneys' property," Nolan says. "And I heard that all of their kids were sick."

"By chance, do they have four kids?"

Nolan nods.

"I saw a family with four kids yesterday when I was leaving

the hospital," she says. "The kids had awful rashes."

"That was probably them. They must be on well water too. And, this pond feeds into Travis Pond."

"Travis? That's the road where all the fire hydrants keep bursting."

"Exactly. And the winery is right up the hill. With all the plant problems they've had, their pond must have also been hit."

"Hit?"

Nolan nods. "I think someone is dumping salt into these ponds."

She coils back. "Salt? Why? Who?"

He looks away, eyes searching. "Too much salt can make you sick, like Ellis. It can give kids and older people rashes, if they are bathing in it. Think about it: if a kid is having a bubble bath, they or their parents might not notice an odd color in the water. If people drink coffee and tea, they might not notice either." His eyes dart back up to look at her. "It hasn't rained in awhile either."

"It hasn't rained since I've been in town."

"Salt sinks. Fresh water floats. If it hasn't rained, salt sits on the bottom. These wells are usually dug deep, so they'd be pulling more salt water."

"How do you know all of this?"

"A lot from cooking, I guess. Mechanical things, like appliances, wear down faster if there's too much salt in the water too."

"Marley's washing machine!"

"Marley?"

"One of our tellers. She lives somewhere out here off of Travis, in her mother's old house. Her mother had an old washing machine and Marley said it broke."

"Interesting…"

"So wait. If a washing machine running with too much salt water wears out faster, that might mean fire hydrants…"

Nolan nods. "Can burst. Salt makes iron corrode faster. Especially the old ones…like around this side of town. Maybe they're not on city water."

Kendra's shoulders shrink. "And all the ones bursting have been up here. They must be corroding from salt! Matt's been chasing around these bursting hydrants and saying something isn't right. I think we need to get him out here." Kendra types a text.

Really need to talk to you. Text when you get back or even better, call.

"He's working?" Nolan asks.

"Yeah, and he can't take his personal cell with him when he's off on a call. New rule from Rip."

"Rip…" Nolan's eyes drift off again.

"What do you think of him? Matt doesn't trust him."

"He's a lousy tipper, from what Gina's told me. I just…I don't know…but in the restaurant I overheard his wife talking to The Betty last week."

"You call her The Betty too?"

He shrugs. "Everyone calls her The Betty. The other day, Gina was busy and their order was ready, so I walked around to the front and delivered it to their booth. I don't know what they were talking about, but Rip's wife Daisy clearly said 'that will get rid of him for good.'"

Kendra's eyes shift. "What day was that?"

Nolan looks up. "Monday? Yeah, it was last Monday."

Monday? Her first day at the bank. The day she cashed The Betty's five-thousand dollar check from Daisy. "What are they up to?"

"They could have been talking about getting rid of a nuisance raccoon for all we know."

"Or…" she says, beginning to pace. "Are they trying to frame someone? Like, Matt? He's made it very clear he wants Rip's job. Rip must be threatened by him. Matt's been trying to expose his waste and spending. He's been worried that if he says more, he'll get fired. Oh God…are they trying to set up Matt?"

"How does salting an entire side of town do that?"

She shrugs when suddenly her phone in her hand vibrates. *Matt?* She looks down. "What…the…heck?" she says, reading the message.

"Who is it?"

"Davis!"

"Davis? He should be off enjoying his honeymoon."

"Well, apparently not anymore." She leans closer to Nolan to show him her phone.

The honeymoon's over. Just got back into town. Susan was called into work for a mandatory emergency meeting tomorrow. Is something going on?

Nolan and Kendra lock eyes.

"The mayor made her come back? What prick makes a bride come back to work two days into her honeymoon?" Kendra asks.

Nolan runs a hand through his hair. "I think we have a few

missing dots to connect. The motive here isn't making sense. We need more information."

She feels his intensity, his focus. "What do we do?"

He breaks their stare. "First, let's go up to the winery. I know the tavern runs on city water but I want to see if they use well water for irrigation and if there are tracks like these around their pond too. If they are, then we should circle the wagons and get more people involved."

"Agreed." She quickly types a reply to Davis.

Not good! I hope the two days you had together were amazing! BRB

Nolan and Kendra open the door back into the house and are greeted by the rotten garbage smell. "I'll get the garbage while you get the lights," she says. While he flips off the garage lights, she puts her phone on the counter, finds a fresh garbage bag under the sink, pulls out the stinky bag and replaces it with a new one.

Nolan waits at the door and in seconds, they're back in the truck heading down the gravel road.

Back on Route 5, Nolan's headlights are the only light on the road, except for the moon's orange glow. The feathery tassels of corn stalks on either side of the road look like wisps of fire in the orange light. But even in this light Kendra sees the crispy bottom leaves of the stalks, row after row.

"Look how dry that corn is," she mutters.

Nolan glances over. "That's Ernie Pratt's land. He must be on well water too."

"And you can't water plants with saltwater, or they'll die," she says. "That has to be the problem at the winery. But how do you know for sure that the tavern isn't on well water?"

"From catering there. The water in the tavern is fine and there's no well pump anywhere around that building."

She looks at him. "Who would have thought that you, and me, would be out doing this now?"

Nolan's dimples appear for the first time tonight, surrounding his warm smile. "I'm not sure anyone else in this town would be up for an adventure like this." He glances over to her and squeezes her forearm. "We have the same curiosity."

She shrugs and sits back in the seat. "Sometimes my curiosity gives me more problems."

More problems: like the day she went to Christopher's medical school bookstore to buy him a diploma frame. She always thought it was strange that he never displayed his diploma, so instead of asking him why, she went to buy him a nice, official frame. In the hallway leading to the bookstore, she stopped to admire the group photos of every graduating class. But for Christopher's year, he wasn't in the picture. When she asked him about it, he said he had been busy that day. He also said he had lost his original diploma. She couldn't leave it alone and set off to "fix" his problem. She went to the registrar's office to order a duplicate diploma, a request which was intercepted by Portia's friend. When Christopher found out she was poking around the registrar's office, he was livid. His reaction, and inconsistencies in his story, eventually led to her discovering the truth. In the end, it was for the best that she left him. But during that time, it sure didn't feel like her curiosity was a friend to her.

"Well," Nolan says, "hopefully our curiosity pays off and helps solve problems."

She nods. That'd be nice if, for once, her curiosity didn't bite her in the ass.

He turns down a dirt road at the bottom of a small hill.

"Is this a secret back way into the winery?" she asks.

"Not really a secret, but most people don't know about it. We'll end up at the tavern this way. We'll park there and see if we can find the pumping station for the winery's irrigation. If we came in the front entrance, someone from the gas station across the street might see us, and I'd rather stay incognito."

Up ahead, the tavern roof appears and Nolan turns off his headlights as he approaches a back parking lot.

"I never noticed this lot when I was here for the wedding," she says.

"It's for deliveries and the catering staff to park in during events, that type of thing." He pulls into a spot in the empty lot.

Kendra looks around. "This is trespassing, isn't it?"

"Pretty much." Nolan grins. "I've been up here enough to know: no one is around at this time of the night."

She dips her chin. "How many times have you been up here at this time of night?"

He grins again. "The winery is a romantic spot, ain't gonna lie. But…I'm usually up here late, hauling away food and supplies after an event."

Sure. At some point after this drama, she's curious to know who—if anyone—he's seeing right now. Hotness like him surely has been claimed.

They get out of the truck and she immediately shivers. "If I had known we'd be traipsing through the woods I would have worn a coat!"

He throws his arm around her and pulls her closer. "Let's

run inside and see if there's a blanket or extra coat."

She leans into him. "Inside? How can we do that?"

He squeezes her. "Have you not even slightly picked up on my outstanding sense of resourcefulness?"

Of course there's a back way in and he knows it. "I'm quickly learning to never doubt you."

They duck under a low hanging wooden trellis. Empty wine barrels line the outside tavern wall and an old picnic bench sits outside a back door. She tries to outsmart him and figure out where a secret key would be hidden. That limestone rock? In the wooden crate over there? Under that nasty bucket?

He reaches for the doorknob, turns it, and opens the door.

"The back door's unlocked? Always unlocked?"

He grins. "Always."

They walk into the tavern kitchen, a small space with deep, stainless steel counters and prep tables. The air is thick with a pungent, musty wine smell. A rack with pots and frying pans hangs over a large stove and the refrigerator looks as wide as her car.

"They sometimes do fire pit nights with wine tastings," he says, opening a closet door and looking around. "And I know I've seen blankets here. They give them away. Ah ha!" He pulls out a red fleece blanket, embroidered with a Cory City Winery logo.

"These are nice," Kendra says, squeezing the fleece. "Of course they spend money on this and give them away..." She wraps herself in the blanket.

"Good?" he asks.

"Great!"

They step out the back door and begin to walk across an

open field that leads to rows and rows of grapevines.

"On the other side of these vines is the pond. My guess is there's a pumping station with some water tanks over there," he says.

The wooden posts are higher than her head, the vines twisted on wire. Even in the dark, with only the moon's light, she can see that the vines look dry. She pulls the blanket tighter. Nolan notices and wraps his arm around her shoulders again. *Gotta admit: he's one hell of a gentleman.*

Nolan stops every now and again to stand on his toes and peer over the vines. "That looks like a water tank down there." He points to the right.

A break finally appears in the long row of vines and the two turn down a narrow gravel road. The gravel crunching under their feet is the only sound. Nolan squeezes her shoulders again. "It's getting cold, huh?"

"Very cold. And I'm thinking of at least two other pairs of boots I have that would have been better for this much walking!"

Nolan glances down at her suede boots. "Every time I've seen you, you're always very stylish."

"Really? Even in my favorite sweatshirt yesterday? The one with the paint smudge on the bottom and the ripped seam on the side that also doubled as my hospital wear?"

"You rocked that sweatshirt even when you were collapsed on the diner floor."

She leans her head closer to his chest. His words seem to make the cold air warmer.

Suddenly, he stops. "Look at that." He drops his arm and points to a group of water storage tanks now visible at the end of the road. A few crunchy steps later, they reach them.

Nolan steps ahead and looks over the equipment. "They've got a well! There's the pump and the water goes to these storage tanks." He reaches for a mechanical box and tugs at the lock but can't jiggle it open. "Gotta be the irrigation controls in here."

Kendra stands beside one of the tanks. "Look how rusted these tanks are."

Nolan examines the bolts, the sides, the base. "Saltwater can easily rust these tanks. How can they not notice this?"

"Now we know there's a well, at least for irrigation."

"So now let's find the pond and see if there are tire tracks." Nolan reaches out his arm and sweeps her closer, steering her back to the gravel road. A few steps later, the rows of vines appear. They can see another gravel road up ahead but instead of walking on the road, they turn down another long row of vines.

Now on the grass, her boots crush the fallen leaves as they walk and the tips of her toes feel frozen by the cold. She's got to keep her mind off of the temperature! "So, have you always lived here?" she asks.

"No, I'm originally from New York."

"Really? Where?"

"The city. Manhattan."

"I would die. I have always wanted to live in a bigger city than Richmond. So, how did you end up here in small town Virginia?"

"Wanted to make my own name for myself," he says, eyes to the ground, watching their feet as they walk. "My dad is fairly well known. He's the chef at a restaurant; a new place called Ink. It's a pretty hot restaurant now."

"I wish I knew more about New York City restaurants. I wish I've *been* to more New York City restaurants!"

"He would have helped me start out anywhere, but I wanted to get out on my own. I know I let him down, not getting good grades in school. By being on my own, I'm proving to myself, and to him, that I can be something. Someday." He squeezes her shoulders, still trying to keep her warm.

What a twist from Christopher's situation. Christopher was pressured by his investment banker father to be a doctor. His father pulled some strings to get Christopher into a good medical school where Christopher tried, and succeeded, for a while. But in his final year of med school, he blew off clinics. He skipped classes. Then he dropped out in his last semester. His mistake was quickly fixed by Portia. Big sister had connections at the medical school and somehow she arranged to have Christopher's records forged. Christopher spent three years working in a doctor's office, while he convinced his father he was off doing a residency. Thanks to Portia's low-life friends, his residency was forged too. Christopher may have been on his own, but he's nothing like Nolan. Christopher had liars boost him up. He's breaking the law. Sure, he has enough knowledge to save lives, like she saw him do tonight. But he has to come clean. He needs to turn himself in. Or stop practicing. This is nothing like Nolan. He's working hard, on his own, to prove to himself that he's worthy of his father's shadow. He's already proved to her that he can be something, someday.

"Well," she says, "from where I sit, which is at the barstool watching you cook, I think you've made a name for yourself. Everyone knows you. Everyone loves your food!"

"Even you?"

"Especially me!"

He squeezes her again. "You're mighty kind there, Kendra,"

he says with a goofy southern drawl.

She playfully leans into him. "Well, you're pretty tasty there, Nolan," she says, trying to mimic his accent.

He drops his arm, stops and faces her with a sassy smile. "Tasty? I'm tasty? That just replaced you liking what I do with my buns as the freshest compliment ever!"

She covers her face, laughing, and then peeks at him from behind her fingers. "Why do I talk like a fool around you?"

He puts his hands in the air, snapping to imaginary music, while they slowly keep walking forward. "I'm tasty. Tasty man. Me, me, me: tasty."

"You are a hot mess is what you are." She tugs her blanket tight again. He's a couple of steps ahead of her, now moving his feet along with his arms to his "tasty" song.

They're almost to the edge of the grapevine row when bright headlights sweep over the vineyard. Nolan stops, eyes wide, and steps back to Kendra, covering her with his arm. They both duck down, leaning closer to the vines to hide.

"Who's that?" she whispers.

Nolan leans down, peeking through the vines. A pickup truck has made the turn near where they are and has come to a stop. "I can't see who that is. But I don't think they see us."

Lights sweep around again as the truck begins to back up. The driver manages to squeeze the truck in backward, in-between two rows of grapevines. He's across the road, a good stone's throw from where Nolan and Kendra stand. The driver turns off the lights and then the ignition.

"They're hiding their truck?" Kendra whispers. "Who comes up here late at night to hide like that?"

Nolan smirks, looks her up and down, and shrugs.

"Oh yeah, us, but besides us," she says.

The truck sits for a minute. There's no movement inside the cab. "Is there one person, or two?" she whispers.

"I can't tell. It better be one. Because if those windows start getting steamy…" he says, turning to her with a raised eyebrow.

She laughs quietly. "Oh my God, we'd be perverts to watch a bouncing truck."

He peers through the vines. "Told you this was a romantic place."

The truck door opens. Kendra and Nolan knock their heads together, both straining to see through the vines.

Someone begins to step out. One cowboy boot stomps on the ground.

A man stands up, his body still partially covered by the open door. His cheek glows from the light of a phone. Even the bright light of tonight's moon and the dim light from the truck's cab isn't enough for Kendra and Nolan to recognize him yet.

"I'm up here now, in position," they overhear him say. "We've got him tonight. And it's about goddamn time."

His free hand reaches around the door and he slams it shut, standing now in plain sight of Kendra and Nolan.

It's Rip Edwards.

[SIXTEEN]

"What's he doing up here?" Kendra whispers, practically cheek-to-cheek with Nolan.

"This town is getting weirder by the minute," he says.

She gently elbows him. "What do we do?"

"Watch him." He nods. "He doesn't see us but we see him. We watch his next move."

Kendra leans back, tightening her blanket. "He said 'we've got him.' Is this an ambush?"

"I'd think the police would be here if it was an ambush, like a drug deal or something."

Her stomach feels sick. "Do you think this has anything to do with Matt?"

"Hard to say," he says, peeking through the vines.

Rip peers out from behind a grapevine row, looking down to the main winery entrance. He turns back and walks to his truck and pulls something out of the back bed. He walks out on the road, closer where they can see him better. He's carrying several skinny, dark strips.

"Whoa," Nolan whispers. "Stingers."

"Are those spike strips?"

They watch Rip walk down the road, unfold a stack of sticks and place them on the road. He picks up handfuls of gravel and scatters it over the sticks.

"Yeah, those are tire shredders. Whoever he's waiting for, he wants to make sure they don't leave."

Rip looks around again, then goes back to sit inside his truck.

"Ever get the feeling you're not supposed to be somewhere?" Kendra asks.

"And we're stuck too." Nolan looks to the right and the left. "We can't walk to the pond because he'd see us in that clearing and that field is too open where we came from, between here and the tavern."

Kendra looks both ways too. "I want to call Matt. I have a bad feeling this is somehow set up for him." She pats her sweater. "My phone! Did I leave it in your truck?"

"I don't think so."

No! "It's at Ellis's house! I left it on the counter when I changed the garbage bag!"

He pats his back jeans pocket. "My phone's in my truck!"

Her shoulders tighten. "Matt could have been calling me! I have no way to warn him! And no one knows where we are. We are completely stuck!"

Nolan peers through the vines again. "We have no choice. We wait."

* * *

Time seems to pass slower than when she is in a face-to-face meeting with Mrs. Danner. Nolan and Kendra sit huddled together on the ground. Kendra sits on half of her blanket, since she's still wearing her work skirt and needed to sit on something other than crushed leaves and dirt. The other part of her blanket wraps up the back of her body to her shoulders. It's only been twenty minutes, but since she's lost all feeling in her nose and kneecaps, it feels like longer.

Nolan has his arms completely around her, one arm holding her back, the other trying to keep her arms warm in front. Her jaw begins to chatter. "Thank you for trying to keep me warm," she stutters.

He adjusts his scarf that he's wrapped around her neck and gently rubs her arms. "Here, maybe that will help. We can't stay out here much longer. You'll freeze."

She rests her head on his chest, her cheek pressing against his flannel shirt, which peeks out from under his leather jacket. He feels soft yet strong. Her eyes drift closed. "You're so warm. Such a tasty and comfy guy," she mumbles.

"You forgot the joke about my buns. Remember? You like what I do with my buns."

Trust: she'll never forget that. "See? Warm, tasty, comfy, buns: you're the whole damn package."

He squeezes her tighter. "Under different circumstances, having you in my arms like this would be a dream come true."

Dream? She gazes up. "Me? A dream come true?"

He doesn't look at her, focusing instead on Rip's truck. "I shouldn't have said that. You have a boyfriend. Sorry. Blame the cold and my frozen brain." He smiles.

She squeezes him. "You're quite a catch yourself, you know. I've never asked you if you have a girlfriend. I mean, after I assumed your sister was your girlfriend I was way too embarrassed to ask."

He says nothing, eyes lost in the distance, staring at the truck.

"Hey," she whispers. "I'm sorry, was that too personal?"

"Huh? No, no. Not at all." He looks down. "I just want to keep you warm. Safe and warm. That's all I want right now."

That's all she wants right now too. Maybe it's the cold. Maybe she's tired, weak. But this feeling, in Nolan's arms, under this moon, even in this odd situation, there's no place she'd rather be. *What's happening to her?* Just this morning, she woke up beside Matt. A few hours ago, she imagined her lips all over Christopher again. Now, she's frozen but blissfully comfortable in the arms of the adorable, gracious and super hot Nolan. *Nolan?* He was never on her radar. Or maybe he was. She noticed him. His jeans. His buns. He made her smile. He made her happy. But she thought he was taken. She assumed someone so edgy and attractive would be. But…he's not? She could have had blueberry pancakes…forever?

Stop. This is crazy. Her emotions switch as fast as if she was flipping through the pages of Cindy's *Red Hot American Men* calendar. *Pick a month; pick a man.* For her, it's more like pick an hour, pick a man. Instead of picking either the doctor, the chef or the fireman, she's acting like she's the spiral binding of a calendar and able to hold them all.

Nolan straightens.

Kendra focuses. "What?"

"We've got company."

Way down by the main winery entrance, a pair of headlights has slowly turned in. Kendra sits up, pulling away from Nolan's arms. He stands and offers her a hand up. Together they peer through the vines to watch Rip.

He gets out of his truck and hides behind the row of vines camouflaging his truck. He too watches down the dirt road. The headlights come closer. Closer.

Her hands go clammy and the hairs on her neck rise. "He put the spikes so far down the road, by the time their tires go flat they'll be right next to him!"

Nolan licks his lips. "Just be ready to run. If something gets weird, run to my truck. It won't matter who sees us at that point. Just run."

Kendra aggressively bobs her head. *Hell yeah she can do that.*

The lights drive closer. Her vision blurs. Cold air has clogged her brain. Fear has taken hold. Lights from the truck blind them as the truck turns to the straightaway, where Rip's sneaky trap lies. She doesn't know if these are bad guys! They could be good guys! She's so confused!

Pop! Pop! Pop! The truck hits the spikes. It slows, limping with flat tires on the road right across from them…right across from Rip…right where he wanted them…and right at the exact moment her world stopped spinning.

The truck.

That truck.

It's Matt's gray Chevy Silverado.

[SEVENTEEN]

"It's Matt!" she whispers. Her pounding heart feels like it's beating in her throat. She turns to Nolan. "Oh my God! Should we warn him Rip is there? I can't stand here and not warn him."

Nolan squeezes her arm and looks back to Matt's truck. "You might want to wait. He's not alone."

Kendra snaps her head to see. A woman opens the passenger door.

"Now what?" the woman with a slight southern accent says, getting out of the truck.

A rush of anger warms Kendra's body. "Susan?" she whispers. "What the hell is Susan doing with him? Up here? At this hour!"

Nolan squeezes her arm tighter, almost to keep her still, or to hold her back from running out and confronting them all.

"All my fucking tires are flat!" Matt yells, walking around to the passenger's side of the truck, the side in clear view of Nolan and Kendra. He slaps the side of the truck.

"Now what, Matt? How will you get this load all the way down there?" Susan asks.

Kendra gulps. Nolan tenses. "Load?" Nolan whispers, squinting.

Suddenly a flashlight shines on Matt and Susan. "Yeah, Matt," Rip says, bursting out from behind the wall of vines and darting to the front of the truck. "How the hell are you gonna get that load down to the pond?"

"Oh my God!" Susan yells, running behind the truck.

"What the hell are you doing here?" Matt yells.

"Catching a crook," Rip says, shining the flashlight into Matt's eyes.

All the anger that had warmed Kendra's blood has now gone cold with shock. Her breath hitches, her knees ready to buckle.

"You're the crook, idiot," Matt says, swatting the flashlight out of his face.

"Let's see." Rip steps past Matt, dashing to the truck bed. Susan runs away from him, to the front of the truck. Rip yanks off a plastic tarp and points his flashlight in the back. His eyes bulge so wide that even Kendra can see them. "You son of a bitch!" He shines the flashlight back in Matt's face.

"Mind your own business, jerk," Matt says.

"We knew it was you," Rip yells. "We thought it was both of you!" He turns the light to Susan, standing terrified at the front of the truck, and then flashes it back to Matt. "You've been stealing road salt! And dumping it in these ponds!" He flashes his light back to Susan. "And you've been the one unlocking the city supply!"

Matt moves closer to Rip. Rip quickly steps back, shining his light in Matt's face. "What the hell is wrong with you, kid?" Rip yells.

"YOU are what's wrong with me," Matt yells. "You cut money

from us at the station but you go and buy yourself anything you want. You should have lost your job a long time ago. Instead, you get richer. The mayor gets richer. The stupid winery owner gets richer. Everyone steals from us and gets richer…except us!"

"What kind of a warped world do you live in?" Rip asks.

"I live in a world where wrongs get righted, old man," Matt says. "You're nothing like my grandfather. Your day has come. This town is falling apart. The press is now asking questions. Finally, someone will hold you accountable for all the years of neglect. The neglect for your personal gain!"

"This town is falling apart because you are poisoning it!" Rip yells.

"You have no proof!"

"What the hell is this?" Rip reaches into Matt's truck bed, grabs a handful of road salt, and throws it at him. "That's salt, son! And it has no business being dumped in these ponds!"

Nolan faces Kendra, still holding her arm. Her heart has imploded. An ache she's never felt before covers her body.

Matt steps towards Rip. "Who said I'm dumping it, huh? Road salt isn't illegal. Who says I can't have it in my truck?"

Rip drags a hand through his hair. "Good God, what's wrong with you? You're going to deny it? You're up here, in the middle of the night, in a place you're not supposed to be, with a truck full of salt and you're going to pretend this is normal? You were about to dump this in that pond! You knew your supply was about to run out! We set a trap…and you fell for it!"

"What?" Susan mutters. "A trap?"

Rip shines his light back on her. "A trap. A brilliant one. Fletcher told everyone yesterday that all road salt would now be inventoried. He knew it would lure you back into town, even on your honeymoon. He knew Matt would panic." Rip shines the light on Matt. "You were about to lose your unlimited supply. The keys weren't going to be in Susan's department anymore. We knew that would force you to make one last dump; one last chance to poison the innocent people of this town!"

Matt jumps at Rip, grabbing his flashlight. He strikes Rip over the head with it, then punches his face. Susan screams. Rip collapses like a fragile stack of sticks to the ground.

Kendra gasps. She shakes off Nolan's arm, fists her hands, marches out from her hiding spot and stomps like a pissed off soldier ready to rip apart the enemy with her bare teeth.

"You asshole!" she yells.

Matt spins around and drops the flashlight, eyes bulging and wide. "Kendra?"

"Kendra?" Susan yells.

"What the hell? Nolan?" Matt says, head shaking, arms dropping to his sides.

Kendra flicks a glance over her shoulder right as Nolan steps in front of her. "Bursting fire hydrants, huh? Salt causes that. You pretend to be the hero, fixing a problem you caused," he says.

Matt stands taller. He looks past Nolan. "Kendra?"

She's not listening; she's bent down to check on Rip, rolling him on his back. He still feels warm and moans slightly. *At least he's alive.* She stands up and glares at Matt. "You asshole."

Nolan steps closer to Matt. "Salt also causes health problems. In children. In older people. Do you take joy knowing that the hospital is overflowing with sick people? People you made sick?"

Matt's cheeks pulse. "Get the hell out of my face."

Kendra stands behind Nolan's shoulder. Matt's eyes are on her, his expression soft. "Why are you here? Baby, you shouldn't be here!"

She raises her chin. "You asshole."

"Stop saying that!" Matt says, his eyes filling with anger. "I'm saving this town! They can't run it! This crisis proves it! Can't you see what's been happening? They can't handle it!"

"Holy shit," Nolan says. "You created a crisis to force the mayor and Rip out!"

Matt shakes his head. "I'd be a much better fire chief than Rip ever was! This town needs leadership, like me! Kendra, baby, you know I should be chief!"

"No, pal," Nolan says. "What you should be is locked up."

Matt fists his hands and takes a wild swing at Nolan. Nolan ducks and darts backward.

"Stop!" Susan screams, still at the front of the truck.

Kendra runs around Nolan to face Matt. His eyes go soft. Sad.

Her lover. Heaven? No, heaven is hell. She slowly shakes her head. Silence covers the winery; the only sounds come from the hum of distant crickets and from Rip, who makes soft groans as he begins to sit up.

Kendra stands inches from Matt's lips. His body tenses, frozen by her stare. The only thing moving now is their blinking eyes.

She leans in, closer to him. She said it once. She said it twice. She said it three times. And she's not finished.

"You…are a fucking asshole." She slaps Matt's face. Susan screams. Matt winces. Kendra's hand stings. Matt clenches his teeth and raises his hand to grab or hit Kendra but she runs.

Nolan pushes Matt in the stomach to force him away.

"Stop!" Matt screams, stumbling backward. Kendra runs around to the front of the truck and Nolan follows. Matt tries to cut them off, running around the other side. Susan runs away from them all, into the rows of vines.

"No! Get back here!" Kendra yells after Susan. "How could you marry Davis, you criminal?" Kendra screams, chasing Susan. "How could you hurt people? Kids?"

Susan glances back, her blonde hair bouncing, arms flapping as she runs away from Kendra.

Bitch. Like, damn! No way you're getting away from me. No way! Kendra runs faster.

"Jerk!" Kendra hears Matt yell, followed by a punching sound. *Nolan!* Kendra stops and turns just in time to see Nolan falling to the ground. *Forget Susan!* She runs back down the row toward him. Vines blur as she runs; every step feels like she's running in slow motion! The end of the row is in sight; she's getting closer to Nolan, who stirs on the ground, struggling to get up. She bursts into the clearing when Matt suddenly jumps out.

"Stop!" he barks.

Her legs grind to a halt. "You're the jerk!" she yells. Matt tries to grab her but she darts away again, around the truck. Matt closes the distance on the other side. "What are you trying to do, Matt?" she yells. "Hit me? Kill me? When does it end? Huh?"

"You've got to understand!" he yells. "I've got to make you understand!"

"Oh I understand! Innocent people mean nothing to you as long as *you* get *your* way!"

Nolan's back on his feet, rubbing his face. She grips one side of the truck bed and Matt's got his hands on the other. *What kind of a trap is this if there are no cops here to arrest him? Is Rip some rogue cowboy, setting this trap and trying to catch him all by himself? Where's the help?*

Suddenly, way down the road at the entrance to the winery, headlights sweep in. Followed by another set. Matt sees the lights and growls. His nostrils flare and a vein in his neck throbs.

Kendra does a double take. It will take them three or four minutes to get up here! They need to hurry! Matt could hurt Nolan again, or her! She can't control him. She can't wait that long!

Matt stares at the approaching cars, then snaps his glare to Kendra.

Then he runs.

He bolts past her and runs into one of the long rows of vines.

And Nolan's on his heels.

"Nolan! No!" Kendra calls, running after them.

Matt sprints in the direction of the tavern and into the open field, Nolan not far behind him.

Matt crosses the field, glancing over to the car lights making their way up the winding road. Nolan runs faster, closing in on Matt.

Kendra bursts into the clearing too. The car lights continue up the hill, heading straight for Matt's crippled truck. *What if the people coming don't see them? What if they don't know they're way down here?*

She can't run faster. Her damn boots are slowing her down and her thigh is throbbing from yesterday's shot! The cold air has iced her lungs and every breath hurts. She could turn and run where the cars are, but she doesn't want to leave Nolan!

Matt hits the parking lot and runs straight for Nolan's truck. He yanks at the passenger door, the back door, and then he runs around the other side. The truck shakes as he tries again and again to open a door. He looks up. Nolan has reached the parking lot.

Run faster!

Matt frantically looks side to side and then bolts to the back door of the tavern. Nolan takes a favorable angle, cutting the distance between them. By the time Kendra reaches the parking lot, the two have disappeared inside.

Kendra ducks under the trellis, runs down the sidewalk and throws open the back door.

"Give up now!" she hears Nolan yell.

She dashes through the kitchen, into the main wine tasting room.

Matt has his hands out, slowly backing into a corner by a bar, gasping.

Nolan stands in the middle of the room, catching his breath.

It's over. It's done. Heaven is cornered in the very place he hates: the winery. Nolan glares at him. "Don't. Move," he says.

Kendra's feet feel wet. No doubt her toenails are bleeding after running in these boots. She takes several deep breaths to warm her lungs and calm her heart. "This can't be happening," she mutters.

Matt stands cornered by the bar, hands still out, shaking his head. "I need to explain…"

"I can't imagine how that idea starts," she quietly says. "The idea to hurt people to bring someone else down just so you can move up."

"What they're doing is wrong!" he says.

"What you did is worse," she says.

Nolan stands quietly between them, watching their exchange.

"You even led me out of the hospital," she says. "You put your arm around me and told me…you told me…to keep moving. You didn't want me to see what you had caused."

Matt shakes his head and lowers his hands. "I don't care about those people. All I cared about was you. Don't you understand? You're all that mattered to me."

"Why would you want to fix bursting fire hydrants…that you caused to break?"

He shakes his head.

"You've been doing this a long time, haven't you? I bet a fire hydrant doesn't corrode overnight, right? How can you…like… look at sick people and know you caused it?"

He keeps shaking his head until finally, he looks down.

There it is. Finally: remorse. His slumped shoulders tell her what she needs to know. It's finally sunken in to him, the magnitude of what he's done. She misread him all along. His right verses wrong. She went along with his fight, to help him prove the truth, to help him fulfill his family legacy. But now, finally, watching him backed into this corner, it looks like he gets it. He's sad. Maybe even sorry. *Oh Matt…*

Then his head rises, firm. "But I wasn't the one who hurt you." His eyes tighten and his shoulders straighten. "I've never hurt you, not like he did." He glares at Nolan.

Nolan lowers his head. "Oh, really?"

"You poisoned her. You could have killed her!" Matt says, pointing at Nolan.

"No, I didn't," Nolan says.

"She ended up in the hospital, because of your stupidity!"

Kendra rolls her eyes. Matt is unhinged! But they've got him cornered. It won't take the others long to find them here in the tavern. Let him talk. Let him babble. The longer he stays in that corner, the sooner this will be over.

"Stupidity?" Nolan asks. "Do we really want to talk here about sending a woman to the hospital because of stupidity? Huh, Matt?"

"Fuck you, Nolan."

"Fuck you, Matt."

Kendra's eyes dart between them. What the hell are they talking about?

"How much longer did you think I'd wait before I told Kendra?" Nolan asks.

"It's none of your business."

"I'm a man, Matt. A gentleman. And no way in hell was I going to stand by and let any new woman in this town be with you for long. At least, not without warning."

"Shut the fuck up."

"Then quit talking about stupidity sending people to the hospital when you know your own damn fist does that."

Kendra straightens with shock. *What?*

Matt tenses. "And again, you don't know the whole story, so just shut up."

Nolan shakes his head. "But I do know the whole story. Brenda sat at my counter and told me. Morning after morning. She sat right where Kendra does now—same barstool. And it was only a matter of time before Kendra started telling the same story."

"You don't know nothing!" Matt says.

"Yes, I do. I was there when she showed up with a bloody lip and nowhere to go. I heard it all. We all helped her."

"You hit your ex?" Kendra says, eyes tightening.

Matt shakes his head.

"Leaving you and this town was the best decision of her life," Nolan says.

Matt's face reddens. He turns and grabs two handfuls of wine glasses from the bar, and throws them toward Nolan. Nolan puts up his hands but can't stop the shower of glasses hurtling his way. Kendra instinctively raises her hands to protect herself too. Glass crashes around Nolan, smashing and cracking. The second she lowers her arms, she finds Matt in her face.

He grabs her, pushing her toward the kitchen. She screams with anger and fury and he throws her against the stainless steel counter. A sharp pain shoots up her back. "Don't believe what he says! He's a punk!" Matt screams. He squeezes her wrists.

"Help!" she screams. He drops her wrists and slaps his hand over her mouth. She punches his face with her free hands. She wriggles and twists and then thrusts her knee into his groin. He cries out, dropping his hold. She runs to the other side of the kitchen. *Shit!* She's cornered! He's near the door, his back to the tasting room. He has the exits! She has nowhere to go! He grinds his teeth with anger.

"Stop, Matt!" she screams, scampering left and then right, searching for something easy to grab in the kitchen to defend herself with. *This is hopeless!*

He slowly walks closer, towering, stalking, angry.

Think! Think! THINK!

Suddenly, relief blankets her.

Got him.

Her shoulders relax.

Oh yes…got him…

She cracks a smile and slowly nods.

He stops, his eyes tightening.

The air in the room feels thick and oddly calm. "Oh, Matt…" she says, grinning.

Confusion twists his face.

"Matt, Matt, Matt…you'll never be the man I'm looking for…" She smirks. "Because no man can be a man, until he knows how to use a frying pan."

Nolan rises up behind Matt and smacks Matt's head with a frying pan.

Matt's eyes roll and he collapses to the floor.

"Bam!" she yells.

Nolan drops the pan and rushes to her. She grabs his arms and he grabs hers. Voices call from outside. The back door bursts open and police rush in. Nolan and Kendra stand face to face in each other's arms, wearing relief and smiles on their faces.

"Are you okay?" he whispers.

She nods. "I'm very good okay."

"Very good okay?" He gently skims his fingertip along her jawline. "You really do talk like a fool around me."

She inches closer, looking over his swollen cheek and the cuts on his unshaven face. *That gorgeous face.* "And I'm very good okay talking like that. To you. Every day. All day."

Her soul feels it, deep inside. It's a click…a deep click she's never felt before. The click of a perfect match. She's eye to eye with the man she's supposed to be with. Her soul mate.

His awesome ass. His quirky jokes. His clever brilliance. His God-blessed amazing food. Burn the hot man calendar. She has what she needs for years to come. She's found her man.

Voices around them demand their attention, but they aren't listening. They just found each other.

Nolan threads his fingers through her hair. His eyes beam bright; his dimples light up the room. She bites her lip. He leans down and slowly, gently, presses his lips on hers. Warmth radiates through her lips, her body, her soul. Tears stream down her face.

Click. Perfect match. She kisses him with intensity, holding his shoulders, as shivers of pleasure cover every inch of her body.

Heaven was good but this…the lips of Nolan Ford… is way better.

[EIGHTEEN]

One Week Later

A late afternoon fire crackles in Kendra's apartment fireplace. She sits barefoot, curled up on the couch in her cozy burgundy velour lounge wear. Her finger gently strokes her big toe, still black-and-blue from last week's run. An open bottle of merlot sits on the kitchen counter; a half-empty glass waits for her to finish it on the end table. She moves her fingers from her toes to stroke the soft velvet of her gray sofa.

Memories of Matt cover every inch of this fabric. His huffing and puffing the night they moved it up, and his naked body the night they broke it in. Every now and then she catches the scent of his citrusy peppery cologne, still woven into the plush fabric. *How will she ever forget him?* She looks to the other side of the sofa and the softer, more emotional memory of him. She drops her hand and gently strokes Gracie's fur.

Gracie rolls her head and looks at Kendra with one open eye. "I love you, girl," Kendra whispers. Gracie yawns.

Her apartment door handle rattles and Gracie snaps to attention. The doorknob turns and Davis walks in, carrying a clear plastic deli bag. "These sandwiches will go with any wine!" He plops the bag on her counter and tilts his head to look at Gracie. "She's still waiting for Matt to come for her, isn't she?"

Kendra strokes her head again. "Yeah. And she's going to be waiting a long, long time." She looks up to Davis. "Your glass is on the counter. Fill it up and let's get this pity party started!"

He looks at the empty glass and then grabs the bottle and takes a long swig.

Kendra shrugs. "Well, okay, you deserve that."

He collapses in a chair across from her, dark circles under his eyes, gripping the wine bottle by the neck. "My divorce will be final by the end of the month."

She shakes her head. "I can't even imagine…"

He slaps his hand on his knee. "I think in the end, it's for the best. I got the feeling Susan wanted a wedding, not a husband. If she could only say no, if she had been strong enough to speak her mind, she might have told me she didn't want to marry me…"

"But she was always so worried about people liking her. She was scared to death of losing friends, which is why she was friends with everyone. She never said no. But she should have, to Matt."

"I thought it was strange when she would go into work late at night sometimes. But she was never gone for that long, so I wasn't really worried. I never thought she was cheating or anything. I never would have imagined this."

"And it was normal for Matt to be out late all the time. Here I thought he was saving people."

Davis shakes his head. "At least she was honest with me when I visited her in jail. She told me she never wanted to unlock the salt supply for Matt. She said she felt terrible every time. But she could never say no…"

Kendra's mind wanders. Maybe Susan had her own motivation. Maybe this was her revenge for the mayor's too-friendly grab that one time. "She could never say no, especially to someone as charismatic as Matt."

"Yeah. You sure can pick them. Speaking of charismatic and your choice in men, heard anything else from Christopher? He left town again, right?"

She rolls her head back. Davis doesn't know the truth. He never knew she ran away from Christopher because he lied about being a doctor. And Davis never knew what Christopher had blackmailed her with. "He texted. He left." She looks back at him. "In some ways, seeing him in the middle of this crisis helped me move on from him. I know—well, he told me—that he's moved on from me."

"And you're okay with that?"

"I am. You know, I saw him in a completely different way, watching him in action. He's good at what he does. But I wouldn't be surprised if he ended up doing something else someday." *Like jail if he keeps this charade up.*

"What would he do?"

"He told me he wants to start his own business. A medical supply business. That would mean he wouldn't practice anymore."

Davis screws up his face. "Why would he go to medical school and all that stuff and then not practice?"

Kendra smiles. "People change. And in Christopher's case, it would be a change for the better."

"You're more relaxed about him, aren't you?"

More relaxed? Sure. Until the day comes when the past

comes out. There's no way he can switch careers and not have the past catch up to him. And someday, the past and what she knew might catch up to her too. "I am more relaxed, about him. I think seeing him, well, it brought the closure I needed."

Davis glances to the counter. "Okay then, ready to eat?"

She shakes her head. "Go ahead. I have no appetite. I just want to get tonight over with." She gently strokes Gracie's head.

Davis looks to Gracie. "Hey, Gracie was lucky you took her in right away, especially since no one in Matt's family wanted her. You made the best decision."

Kendra squeezes Gracie's fur. "I just want her to know I love her."

"I think she already knows."

A knock sounds on the door. A dog barks from outside it.

Gracie snaps to full attention and leaps off of the sofa, running to the door, barking.

Kendra gets up and opens the door. A barking golden retriever rushes into her apartment. Gracie and the retriever sniff and bark and greet each other in a tail-wagging fit.

"Toby!" Rip calls out, quickly running in behind him.

"Don't worry, they can't hurt anything," Kendra says.

"Kendra, hello," Daisy says, following Rip into Kendra's apartment and giving her a hug. "How are you doing, my dear?"

Kendra squeezes Daisy's arms. "I'm fine, really. A little sad about tonight though."

Gracie and Toby romp together on the living room rug. Rip looks at them and then back up to Kendra. "We're happy to take Gracie. She and Toby always got along so well when Matt used to bring Gracie up to the station. She's going to fit right into our family."

Kendra nods. She knows. She wipes a stray tear from the corner of her eye. "I'm really not a dog girl and who knows when Matt will get out of jail to take her back…"

Daisy nods. "I know. It's terrible. But when he does get out, Gracie will be here for him."

Kendra sniffs. "I'm sorry, I didn't introduce you to Davis. You remember him from the wedding, right?"

Davis shakes their hands, still holding the wine bottle by the neck in his other hand. Daisy points to the bottle and nods. "I'd be doing the same thing if I were you."

Davis hoists up the bottle. "Hey, at least I wasn't jilted at the altar. I was jilted two days into the honeymoon when she was arrested, but we made it to the altar."

Daisy nods. "It's okay, honey. If you need to drink, just keep drinking."

Kendra laughs. She can't forget the image of Daisy, an empty glass and bottle of wine in front of her, tipsy at Davis and Susan's wedding. "There's some good advice," Kendra says. "Hey, how's your head, Rip?"

He rubs his hair. "I get a little dizzy sometimes, but I'm fine. I should be able to drive in a week or so. That was some hit to the noggin I got."

Kendra nods. "We all got a little bruised that night. I'm glad you're okay though."

Gracie runs up to Daisy and rubs her nose in Daisy's hand. She squeezes Gracie's head. "Baby, we're going to love you, love you, love you," she mumbles in baby talk.

Kendra clutches her chest.

"You know," Rip says, looking to Kendra. "This whole thing has, well, humbled me a bit. Honestly, Matt was right. Maybe I haven't made the best decisions for the department. Sometimes, I did buy things I shouldn't have. And I'm going to change some things and involve more of the guys when we have money to spend, so we can spend it on the right things."

"If you don't mind me asking, I'm curious about something Matt mentioned," Kendra says. "You all raised money for a new playground but it hasn't been built yet. Where's that money now?"

"It's still in the city fund," Rip says. "They say we've raised enough for all of the new equipment but the lawyers said it can't be built until there is a fence around the entire area. Now we need another fundraiser for the fence! Did he think those funds were used for something else?"

"It doesn't matter now," Kendra says. "Matt had good intentions, you know. He wanted taxpayer money spent right."

"He did. And it will be," Rip says. "And then, one day soon, I will retire. These bones of mine ache after being hit in the head with a flashlight, so I don't know how much longer I can keep this up."

Gracie and Toby race each other around the kitchen. "We should leave now, papa, before these dogs tear up Kendra's apartment. And the mover is coming in an hour," Daisy says.

"You're moving?" Davis asks.

"Oh no," Daisy says, smiling. "But we hired a mover to properly pack and transport a beautiful Howard Miller grandfather clock I just bought from Betty Fletcher."

"The Betty?" Davis asks.

"Yes! It's been in her family for years. She had wanted to sell it but she had been harassed by a rather nasty antique collector. He kept offering her half of what it was worth! Since I am a collector of Howard Miller pieces, I was thrilled to purchase it!"

Kendra squints. *Howard Miller? Clocks like that run in the thousands. Maybe…five thousand?*

Daisy smiles. "So once we get that beautiful clock home, I'm never selling it and we'll get that nasty man out of Betty's life for good!"

"Yes, dear," Rip says.

Get him out of their lives for good? That's what Nolan overheard the ladies say at the diner! It wasn't Matt or some raccoon they were trying to get rid of. It was a pushy antique collector!

Kendra takes a big breath in and reaches for a bag. "Here are Gracie's favorite toys and a bag of her food." Tears begin to fill her eyes. "You know her vet, right? All of her records are there. She loves to sleep under the bed…and she's not a fan of country music…"

Rip pats Kendra's shoulders. "She's with Toby…she's going to be fine."

Kendra gives him a hug and Daisy too. Davis shakes their hands goodbye. Kendra opens the door and Toby and Gracie run into the hall, nipping at each other's tails. Rip and Daisy follow.

Daisy turns back with a gracious smile. "I would still like to go with you to the winery for a tour sometime," she says.

Kendra sniffles. "I would love that." *Except, no need to tour the kitchen. That's one place she never needs to see again.*

Rip and Daisy turn to walk away, Toby and Gracie scampering beside them. Her heart feels stabbed with every step she watches Gracie take away. Suddenly, Gracie turns and with her tail wagging, she runs back to Kendra. Gracie lowers her head. Kendra squats to pet her.

"Your daddy loves you, you know that?" Kendra says, rubbing Gracie's ears and struggling to see through her tears.

"One day, he'll come home and you'll go for walks and rides and all of the things you used to do together, okay?" She wipes her face on the arm of her lounge jacket. "I'm going to come up to the station and visit you, okay? You be a good girl, though, alright? Be a good girl and I'll bring you some of Nolan's brisket."

"Woof!" Gracie barks.

Kendra smiles and stands. Gracie turns and with a wagging tail runs up to Toby. "Woof!" Toby barks, looking back to Kendra. Rip and Daisy smile warmly and walk away.

Kendra closes the door, leans against it and closes her eyes. *Hardest. Thing. Ever.* She opens her eyes to see Davis across the room, chugging hard from the bottle of wine. He comes up for air, tears rolling down his face. "Holy crap, that was harder for me to watch than seeing Susan at the jail."

Her heart feels shredded. That's the last piece of Matt she needed to get rid of, for her to move on. She glares at the sofa. Well, maybe there's one more piece…

She reaches for a box of tissues, wiping her eyes and blowing her nose. She points to the sofa. "Do you remember the night we moved that up here?" Davis nods. "I had to wipe off the legs of that sofa because his truck was so dirty. Remember how dirty the inside of Matt's truck always was? Never the outside, but the truck bed was always dirty."

"It was probably dust from the road salt," Davis says.

God how could he have done this…

Davis hoists the bottle up again for another swig. At this rate, he'll be in no condition to navigate the apartment staircase and need to spend the night on her sofa.

He steps towards the kitchen counter, puts the wine bottle down, and sighs.

"You alright?" she asks.

"Actually, I am," he says. "But I wanted to make sure you were okay first."

"What do you mean? I'm fine…all things considered."

"You might not be after what I'm about to tell you."

Oh geez. What now? What could possibly be worse than what she's just been through?

"Do I need to sit down?" she asks.

"Yeah."

She picks up her wine glass and sinks into the couch. "Hit me."

He falls into the chair across from her, no bottle in hand this time. "This has been the craziest week of my life, with a wedding, a honeymoon being cut short, Susan being arrested and everything…"

Kendra nods. *Preach.*

"And you're not going to believe what else happened," he says.

This must be a silly joke or something! He…got a hangnail. Or he…bought a new sports car. "I can't even guess…what?"

"I got a new job."

"Whoa! Great! How? What? You just moved here! Hold on, you're moving, aren't you?"

He smiles and nods.

Well, he works for a hotel in Richmond and was driving an hour to-and-from his apartment in Cory City just because of Susan. So it makes sense that he would want to be in Richmond, closer to his new job. Assuming his new job is in… "Wait. Where's your new job?"

His smile stretches. "Tampa."

"Florida? Tampa? Who do you know there?"

"Only one person! A friend a little older than me that I went to college with, Lauren Logan. When this job popped up in my business network feed, I thought about her and I applied. I had a phone interview and got it!"

Kendra feels slapped, but by good news. "What will you be doing?"

"Operations director for a resort hotel there. The Riverside Resort."

"Sounds fancy!"

"I'll be working for Lauren's husband, the Vice President of Operations, a nice guy named Cory."

"You're leaving Cory City to go work for a guy named Cory."

"Well, stranger things have happened."

Here? Um, yeah.

Kendra glances over to her wine glass. She's going to need a stiffer drink.

"What a fresh start for you. With what you've just been through, to have a job like that fall into your lap. I'm going to miss the hell out of you though."

He smiles. "I doubt any job in Tampa will have as much drama as what I just had here."

She nods. *Yeah, probably not.*

"You'll visit me?" he asks.

"In Tampa? Hell yeah. Book me for a visit every winter!"

"I already know what my first paycheck splurge is gonna be," he says, looking down to his feet. He wiggles his well-worn loafers.

"Oh no, no," she says, shaking her head. "Not blue boat shoes?"

"Told you I always wanted a pair." He smirks. "And you won't be there to stop me." He gives a happy, sad smile. And her heart feels happy, sad too.

"Davis Perkins is going to Tampa. Why do I have a strange feeling that bigger and better things are in store for you?"

He shrugs. "Because I think bigger and better things are in store for us both."

Deep.

He slaps his hands on his thighs. "Too much wine. Let me hit your bathroom."

He walks away and she stares at her wine glass. She's lost Matt. Tonight, she lost Gracie *and* Davis. If life is burnt toast like Nolan once said, then it feels like she's burning through bread left and right.

She hears a flush and then Davis cries out, "Oh Kendra!?" He flings open the bathroom door and steps into the living room. "Well, my dear, do you mind explaining this?"

He thrusts up a toothbrush.

She grins.

He smirks. "It was right next to the man's razor, in plain sight in your bathroom." He taps his foot.

"What? He needs a place to shave and brush his teeth in the morning. Right?" She acts shy, hiding behind her glass of wine. Then she takes a sip.

Davis nods. "And off you go again, moving fast. I can't imagine you any other way."

"Fast, yes," she says. "But this time, my friend…this time, I think I got it right."

"Right?"

"Bigger and better things for us both, right?" she says, smiling.

"You got that right."

[NINETEEN]

Two Months Later

Bright blue sky covers this clear, cold December day. Steam from a distant smokestack rises in the sky, just across the river from Route 5. Kendra steers her car into a turn, a part of the road so familiar, it doesn't matter anymore if the morning sun blinds her. With both hands on her steering wheel, she uses her thumb to press the volume up button. *This* song deserves every amp that her speakers can give it. She sings loudly, and sort of off-key, to one of her favorite seventies hits of all time: *I Will Survive.*

She pumps the breaks, taking a tight right turn and coming in hot to the Seven Spoons parking lot. *Hope no one saw that.* She swerves around the potholes in an evasive maneuver she's memorized, always careful to avoid "Big Bob"—the name she's given to the massive pothole always filled with water. Her Audi glides into her favorite space just as the best part of the song comes on. Her hands fly up in the air while she scream-sings the lines until finally she drops her hands, stops singing, and puts the car in park. And she doesn't care if anyone saw *that.*

She swivels the rearview mirror to check her makeup and touches up her ruby red lipstick, the perfect shade to match her red Maggie London fit and flare tweed dress. She straightens the mirror and does her usual visual inventory of the cars and trucks in the parking lot. The guys are all here, even Ellis, who once again has mostly missed parking his silver sedan within the lines of the disabled space. She squints. She's on to him though. After seeing how perfectly he parked his car in his own garage, there's a really good chance he's parking like this just for attention. Especially since she teases him about it every day. She squints again. Way over on the side of the dry cleaners next door is a black Volvo like her dad drives. *Good reminder: she owes him a long phone call soon.* A quick tug of the belt on her Ralph Lauren black wool coat and she opens the car door, throwing her Louis Vuitton over her shoulder and firmly planting her feet on the asphalt. "So Kate, meet the world," she says to herself, looking down at her new "So Kate" Christian Louboutin black pumps. She slams her car door shut and swings her hips with confidence with every step toward the door. And she also swings her hips because she knows who's watching her.

The fingerprint-smudged glass door opens with a jingle and she steps into another one of her favorite songs. "No way!" she says when she hears *Dancing Queen* playing.

"Yes way!" Bobby says, looking as scruffy as usual, sitting at his regular round table, spreading jelly on his toast. "You gonna be my dancing queen, baby?" he calls out.

She dips her shoulder. "You bet." She winks at him, takes off her coat, hangs it on the coat rack and glances ahead.

Nolan's busy at the grill, a burst of steam from something he's cooking rising up near his face. He's got his navy baseball cap and a blue t-shirt on and today, he's tied a red and blue checked flannel shirt around the waist of his jeans. She winks at him, even though his back is turned. She knows he can see her. He's looking at her from the shiny back of a frying pan, hanging over the griddle.

"Morning, my love," Gina says, giving her a hug.

Kendra squeezes her back. "Did you finish your quilt last night?"

Gina steps back. "Yes! And it's beautiful! So worth all the problems I had with getting the corners laid down right. Thanks for coming over to help me."

Kendra squeezes her shoulders. "Anytime."

Gina turns to refill some drinks. A cat call whistle sounds from the corner of the restaurant.

"Show me those shoes!" Marvin calls out.

Kendra strikes a pose with her foot pointed out. *These guys would die if they knew how much these were.* Before she walks over to visit with them, she glances up at Nolan again. He's smiling, she can tell from the crease in his eyes, still looking at her from the back of the frying pan. Let him wait a little longer…

She walks to the corner booth to visit with Marvin and Glen, her heels making empowered clicking sounds on the porcelain tile.

"So, here's Marvin's problem for today," Glen says, fiddling with his fingers.

"Big problem," Marvin says.

Kendra points to Glen's shirt. "Let me guess. Glen's wearing orange and you have a problem with that."

Marvin slaps the table. "See! Ha! It's December! You never wear orange in December! Everyone knows that."

She glares at Marvin. "But I didn't say I had a problem with that."

Glen slaps the table. "Ha! Once again my brother proves he has no idea about modern fashion."

She glares at Glen. "But I didn't say it was okay either. I mean, orange?"

Jay, the man in the booth beside them, looks up from his crossword puzzle. "What's an eight-letter word for ordinary person that begins with a p?"

Marvin points to Glen. "PerhapsU?"

Glen points to Marvin. He shakes his finger and then drops it. "Ah crap, I've got nothing."

"Easy one today, Jay," Kendra says. "It's plebeian."

Jay looks down and writes in his puzzle. "Plebeian! Perfect. Thanks!"

Kendra glances over to Ellis. His smile stretches his face, his cheeks warm with color. "Morning over there," she says, coming closer to him. "Couldn't park straight in your space again today, huh?" She leans down to give him a hug. He's warm, cuddly warm, with his fuzzy blue cardigan sweater. "It's a special day today, isn't it?" she says, smiling. He nods, smiling so happy and proud. She leans down again and gives him a kiss on the cheek. "Happy anniversary. I bet Millie is blowing you kisses from heaven."

"Oh I think she would be, that's for sure," he says, looking up and blowing a kiss into the sky.

Kendra lays a hand over her heart. And then her tummy growls.

"Behave back here, boys. It's always a pleasure to visit you."

Glen smirks. "We know it is."

She swats his shoulder as she passes.

Gina's holding a coffee pitcher and turns sideways to let Kendra pass. "I hope you're real hungry this morning," Gina says, adding a wink.

Oh boy. Wonder what that means?

Kendra slides onto her favorite barstool, intentionally sitting with her legs off to the side. She slowly crosses her legs, knowing he'll notice them and her hiked-up dress once he turns around. Nolan's busy flipping sausages on the right side of the griddle. She leans left and then right to see what he's cooking but he's blocking her view. Also blocking her view is his flannel shirt tied around his waist. She'd rather be watching his hot ass at work than looking at that plaid shirt.

She clears her throat. "I sure would like to see what you do with your buns, if only I could see them today…"

He turns his head, resting his chin on his shoulder. His smile burns hotter than his griddle, making the butterflies roar in her empty stomach. His hair peeks out from under his baseball cap and it looks just as messy as when she had her hands all over it earlier this morning. "Good morning," he says with a sultry voice and lowered eyes.

"Yes, it was." She smiles, biting her lip.

He wipes his hands on a towel hanging from his waist. "Hungry?"

"For food? Sure. Other than that, I'm very satisfied."

He glows.

"I've got something special for you, on this special day," he says, turning back to his griddle.

Special day? Her brain races. It's Ellis's wedding anniversary—she remembered that. It's not their anniversary. Nolan's birthday isn't until February. What's today? There's nothing else special about today, right?

Nolan turns and pushes a steaming hot, heart-shaped blueberry pancake her way.

"I absolutely love it!" she says. "Very special. From a very special guy."

He blushes.

Over her shoulder, she notices Glen and Marvin moving near the cash register.

Nolan's eyes light up like a little boy on Christmas day. *What's he up to?* He nods like he knows a secret and starts shaking his arm. He's got a can of whipped cream! He turns the can upside down and squirts a dollop of whipped cream on her pancake.

"Super deluxe special," she says, dipping her chin.

"Oh yeah, baby," he says. His eyes reek of mischief. He raises his chin in the air, parts his lips and squirts whipped cream into his mouth. His eyes lower to look at her as he slowly licks his whipped-cream-filled lips.

She's about to fall off of her chair. *What a mess! A sexy, whipped cream mess!* God she loves every quirky, fun and smart inch of this man. The two of them can have serious discussions, like investment strategies to save money for their imaginary mountain cabin. Then minutes later, they're ripping out the pages of her fashion magazines and having a paper airplane war. Her dreams couldn't dream up a better man than Nolan.

She glances over her shoulder. Gina's standing behind her. Bobby has also gotten up to watch Nolan's whipped cream and pancake show. Marvin and Glen loiter by the register and now even Ellis is shuffling closer to watch.

She spins around to face her whipped cream lover. "Look at this, you're causing a scene."

"Good," he says, beaming. He looks down to her pancake. She follows his eyes.

On top of the whipped cream sits a sparkling silver diamond ring.

Her eyes fly open. She grabs the counter and teeters on her stool. Time stops.

He leans over the counter, closer to her. "I want to cause a scene with you every day…every day for the rest of my life," he says, eyes intense. "Since the first day you sat on that stool I knew you were the one. Baby, I know that we've just started. I know we've got a long way to go. But I want you to know… Kendra, I'm gonna love you just as much in a year as I do right now and I'm not gonna wait until then to show you. Build a life with me…"

His words float around her, surreal. He speaks exactly what she feels. He's channeling her soul, her thoughts, her dreams. She's imagined the same thing too, but never thought this was the time. Is he asking her to…is he really about to…

"Kendra King, will you marry me?"

Her breath is gone. She's pretty sure she just heard everyone behind her suck in their breath too.

The dollop of whipped cream is melting from the heat of the pancake and this moment.

She takes a deep breath and exhales. "I really think I could marry you anytime, anyplace, when we're ready, whenever that is. You bet my answer is yes!"

"Yay!" The onlookers cheer and clap. His dimples crease. He leaps up and over the counter to face her, gently cupping her head. "I can't wait to spend the rest of my life listening to you talk to me like a fool."

Happiness makes tears fall from her eyes. "I love you, Nolan."

His lips come closer. "I love you, Kendra."

He squeezes her cheeks and kisses her as wild applause and cheers surround them. They kiss, again and again. She feels like she's floating; she's losing her mind. She smells something burning from the griddle and is vaguely aware of someone rushing to finish cooking whatever it was. Her lips are on her man. She hears a blur of voices around her.

"About time!"

"I better get invited!"

"It's getting hot in here!"

"Congratulations, Kendra!" she hears a man's voice say.

She stops kissing Nolan, eyes wide. *That voice.* Nolan grins and gently spins her and her barstool around. *Her dad! And mom!* Her parents rush forward and wrap her in hugs. Nolan leans in too, making Kendra the center of a human hug sandwich.

Behind the counter, champagne bottles pop open and glasses are passed out. Music plays and people laugh. Smiles surround Kendra and Nolan. She's never felt this much love; never been so happy.

It took running away from a doctor and drama with a fireman for her to find what she was looking for.

The chef. Nolan Ford. The love of her life.

The End

About the Author

Debbie Krueger Lum has enjoyed a 28-year professional career in marketing, where she loved turning big, complicated problems into smooth, organized programs. She's traveled from the beaches of Turkey to the volcanoes in Italy to the bricks of Red Square, Moscow. And no one can drink more unsweetened iced tea than her.

After seeing a self-esteem campaign encouraging little girls to dream big, she wondered why not grown women too? She challenged herself to do something she knew little about: reading and writing novels.

The Doctor, the Chef or the Fireman is her fourth novel.

www.debbielum.com

Books by Debbie K. Lum

The Plebeian Series
Want to know what happens next to Davis Perkins?
Find out in the Plebeian series.

PLEBEIAN REVEALED (Book One)

When Lauren Logan, in introverted wife and mother, records a secret movie soundtrack with her ex-boyfriend, she gets more than sudden fame when their band Plebeian is revealed.

PLEBEIAN IN DANGER (Book Two)

Lauren thought her stage fear would be her largest challenge during Plebeian's world tour. But a series of bad luck as given her bigger problems. The world tour is unraveling and it's all according to plan. By the time Lauren discovers the enemy within, she's already fallen into a trap. Now she must face a killer to stop this, and resist his love.

PLEBEIAN REBORN (Book Three)

Lauren has survived remarkable challenges as the lead singer of Plebeian. Now she faces her biggest challenge yet—her mistakes from the past. When tragedy strikes and secrets are revealed, she unravels in a downward spiral. Only one man can save her, and Plebeian, now. And it's not her husband.